JUST BEYOND™

VOLUME 1:
THE SCARE SCHOOL

Written by
R.L. Stine

Illustrated by
Kelly & Nichole Matthews

Lettered by
Mike Fiorentino

Cover by
Julian Totino Tedesco

Just Beyond created by
R.L. Stine

Designer
Scott Newman

Assistant Editor
Michael Moccio

Editors
Whitney Leopard
Bryce Carlson

ABDOBOOKS.COM

Reinforced library bound edition published in 2021 by Spotlight, a division of ABDO, PO Box 398166, Minneapolis, Minnesota 55439. Spotlight produces high-quality reinforced library bound editions for schools and libraries.
Published by agreement with KaBOOM!

Printed in the United States of America, North Mankato, Minnesota.
042020
092020

THIS BOOK CONTAINS
RECYCLED MATERIALS

kaboom!™

BOOM! Studios, 5670 Wilshire Boulevard, Suite 400, Los Angeles, CA 90036-5679.

Library of Congress Control Number: 2019955568

Publisher's Cataloging-in-Publication Data

Names: Stine, R.L., author. | Matthews, Kelly; Matthews, Nichole, illustrators.
Title: The scare school / by R.L. Stine; illustrated by Kelly Matthews, and Nichole Matthews.
Description: Minneapolis, Minnesota: Spotlight, 2021. | Series: Just beyond; volume 1
Summary: Drake, Buddy, and Leeda are trying to escape from their school of horrors, but they are pursued by a deadly creature stalking the hallways.
Identifiers: ISBN 9781532144899 (lib. bdg.)
Subjects: LCSH: Middle school students--Juvenile fiction. | School buildings--Juvenile fiction. | Monsters--Juvenile fiction. | Supernatural--Juvenile fiction. | Fear--Juvenile fiction. | Graphic novels--Juvenile fiction.
Classification: DDC 741.5--dc23

ABDO
Spotlight
A Division of ABDO
abdobooks.com

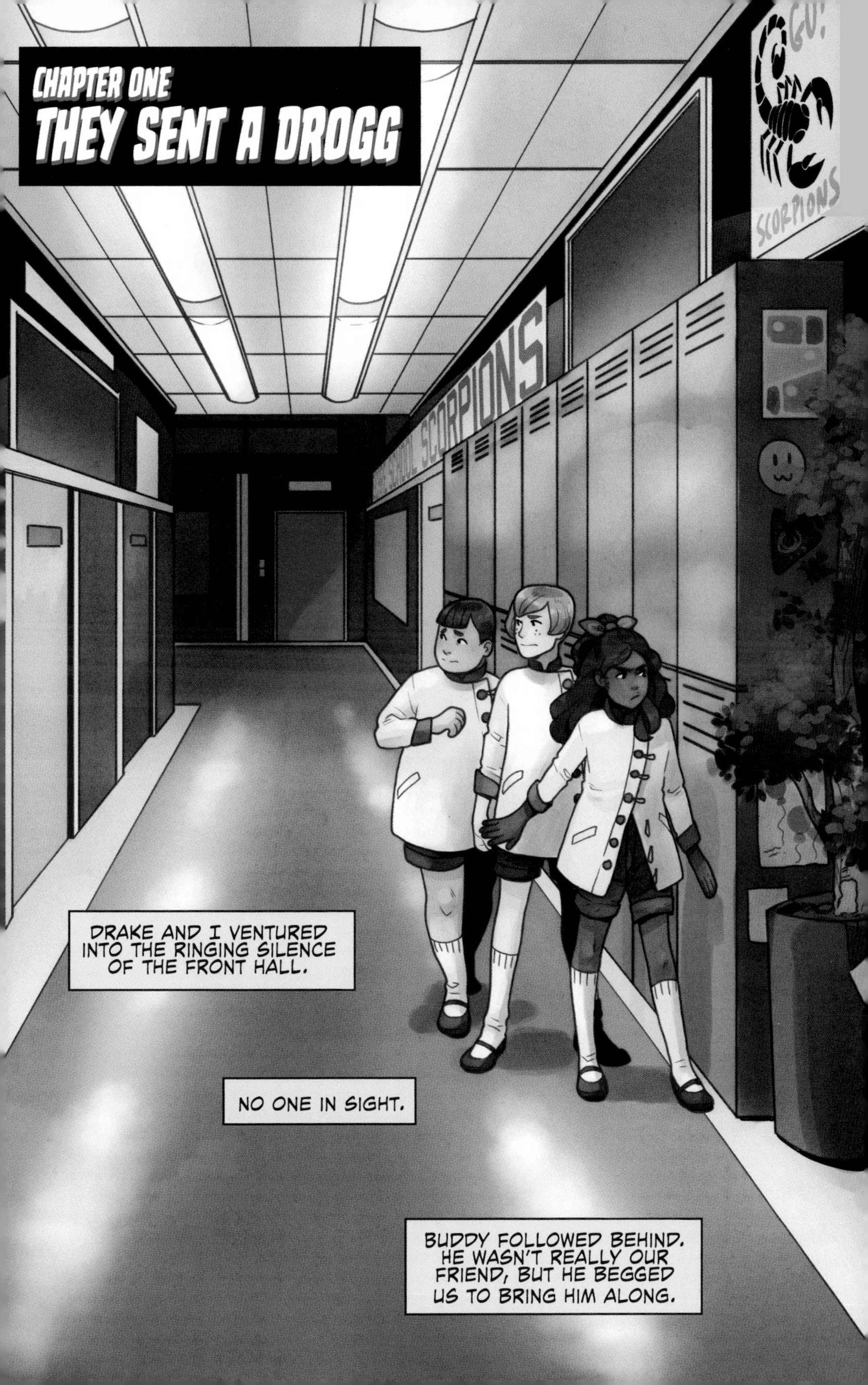
CHAPTER ONE
THEY SENT A DROGG
SCORPIONS
SCHOOL SCORPIONS
SCORPIONS
DRAKE AND I VENTURED INTO THE RINGING SILENCE OF THE FRONT HALL.
NO ONE IN SIGHT.
BUDDY FOLLOWED BEHIND. HE WASN'T REALLY OUR FRIEND, BUT HE BEGGED US TO BRING HIM ALONG.

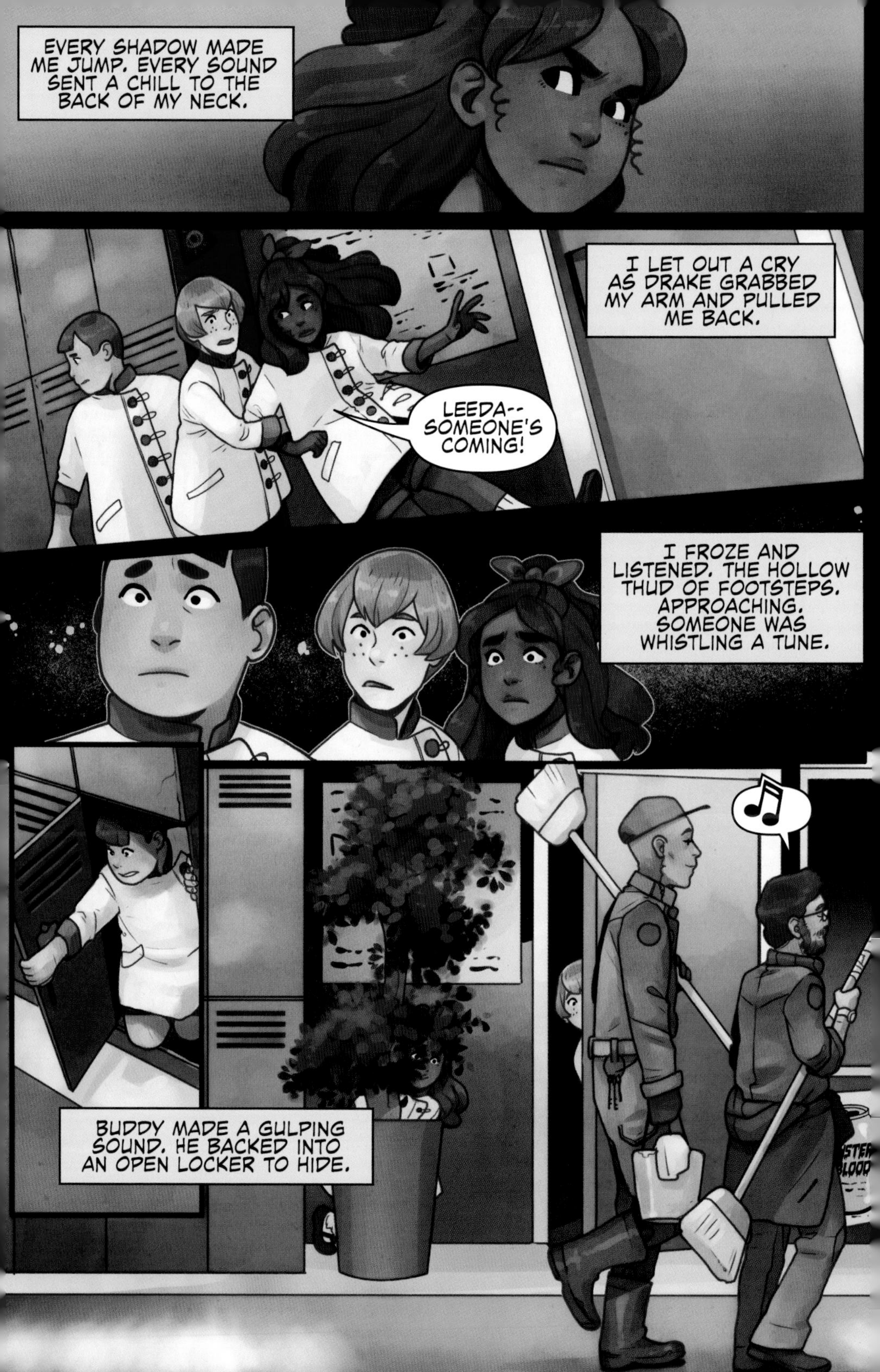
EVERY SHADOW MADE ME JUMP. EVERY SOUND SENT A CHILL TO THE BACK OF MY NECK.
I LET OUT A CRY AS DRAKE GRABBED MY ARM AND PULLED ME BACK.
LEEDA-- SOMEONE'S COMING!
I FROZE AND LISTENED. THE HOLLOW THUD OF FOOTSTEPS. APPROACHING. SOMEONE WAS WHISTLING A TUNE.
BUDDY MADE A GULPING SOUND. HE BACKED INTO AN OPEN LOCKER TO HIDE.

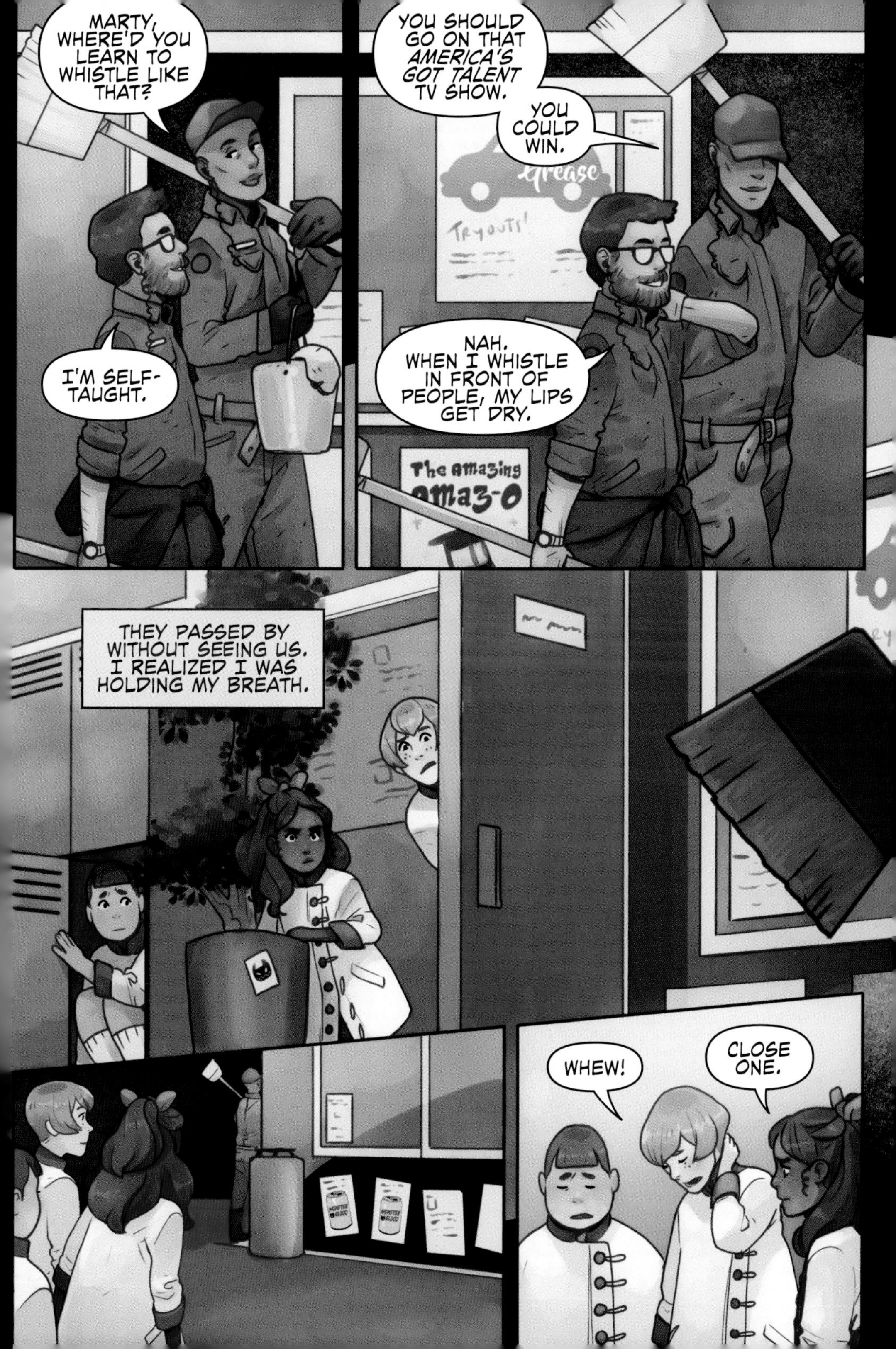
MARTY, WHERE'D YOU LEARN TO WHISTLE LIKE THAT?
I'M SELF-TAUGHT.
YOU SHOULD GO ON THAT *AMERICA'S GOT TALENT* TV SHOW.
YOU COULD WIN.
Grease
Tryouts!
NAH. WHEN I WHISTLE IN FRONT OF PEOPLE, MY LIPS GET DRY.
The amazing Amaz-O
THEY PASSED BY WITHOUT SEEING US. I REALIZED I WAS HOLDING MY BREATH.
WHEW!
CLOSE ONE.

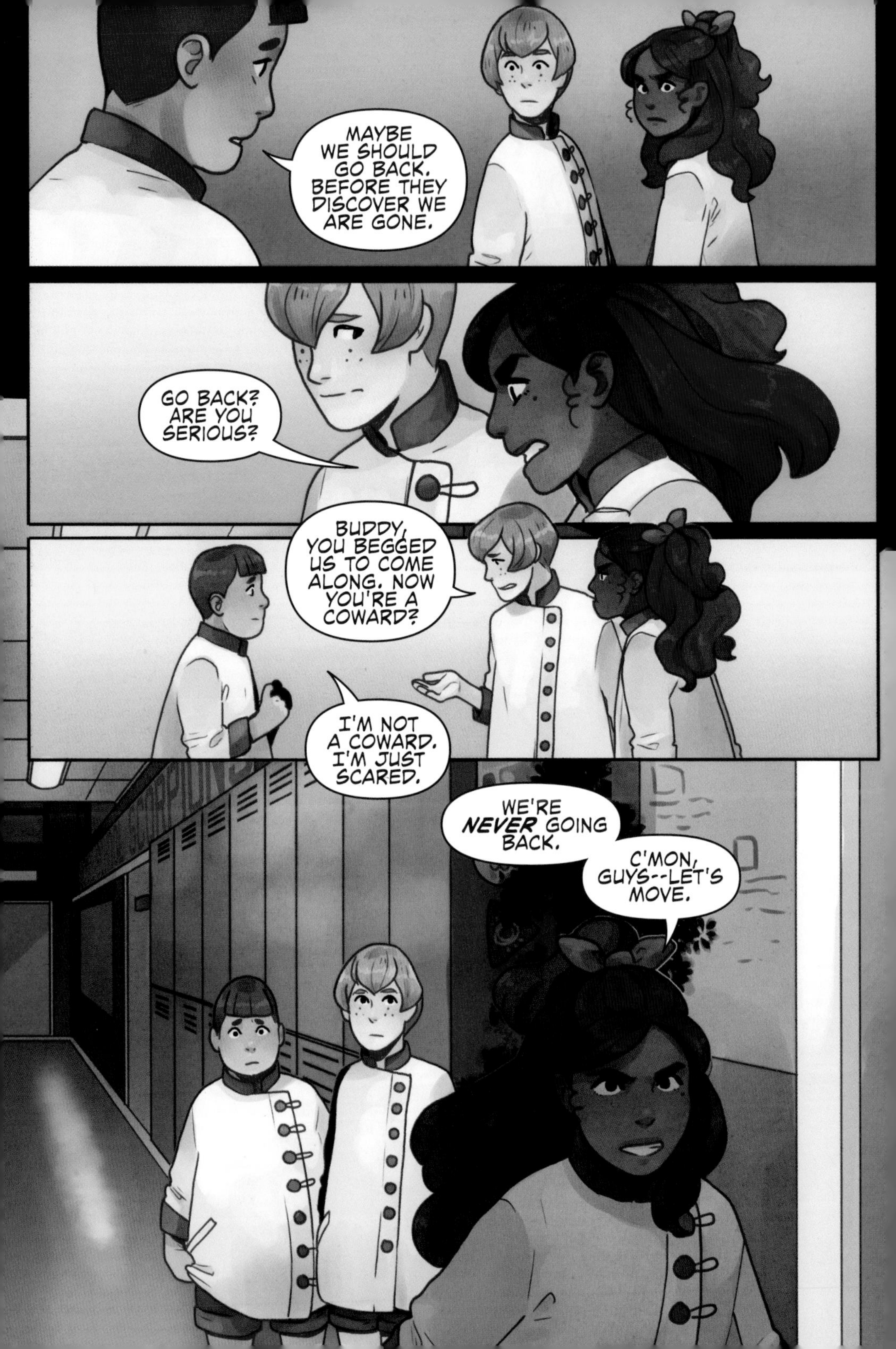
MAYBE WE SHOULD GO BACK. BEFORE THEY DISCOVER WE ARE GONE.
GO BACK? ARE YOU SERIOUS?
BUDDY, YOU BEGGED US TO COME ALONG. NOW YOU'RE A COWARD?
I'M NOT A COWARD. I'M JUST SCARED.
WE'RE *NEVER* GOING BACK.
C'MON, GUYS--LET'S MOVE.

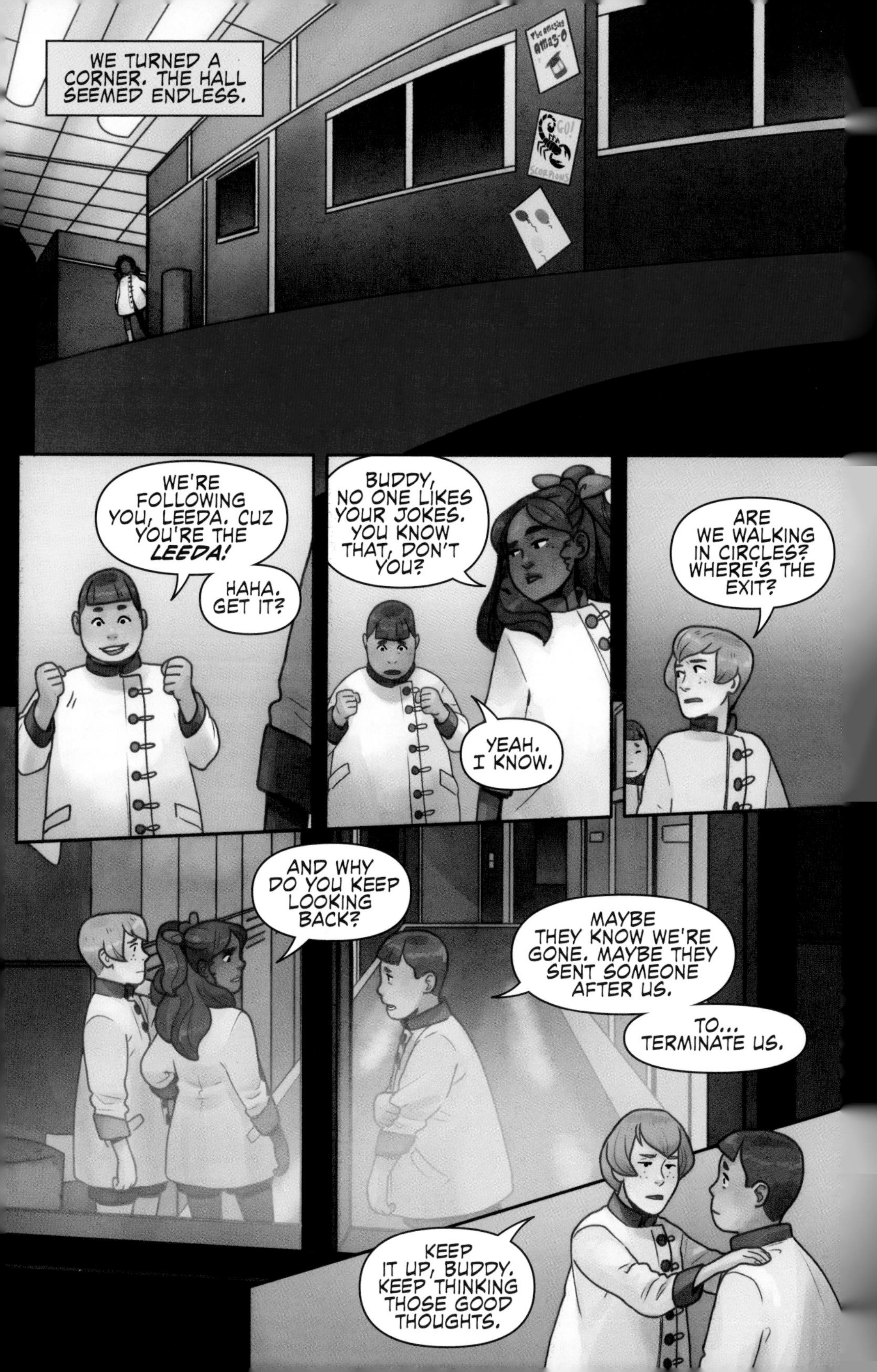
WE TURNED A CORNER. THE HALL SEEMED ENDLESS.
The amazing AMAZ-O
GO! SCORPIONS
WE'RE FOLLOWING YOU, LEEDA. CUZ YOU'RE THE *LEEDA!*
HAHA. GET IT?
BUDDY, NO ONE LIKES YOUR JOKES. YOU KNOW THAT, DON'T YOU?
YEAH. I KNOW.
ARE WE WALKING IN CIRCLES? WHERE'S THE EXIT?
AND WHY DO YOU KEEP LOOKING BACK?
MAYBE THEY KNOW WE'RE GONE. MAYBE THEY SENT SOMEONE AFTER US.
TO... TERMINATE US.
KEEP IT UP, BUDDY. KEEP THINKING THOSE GOOD THOUGHTS.

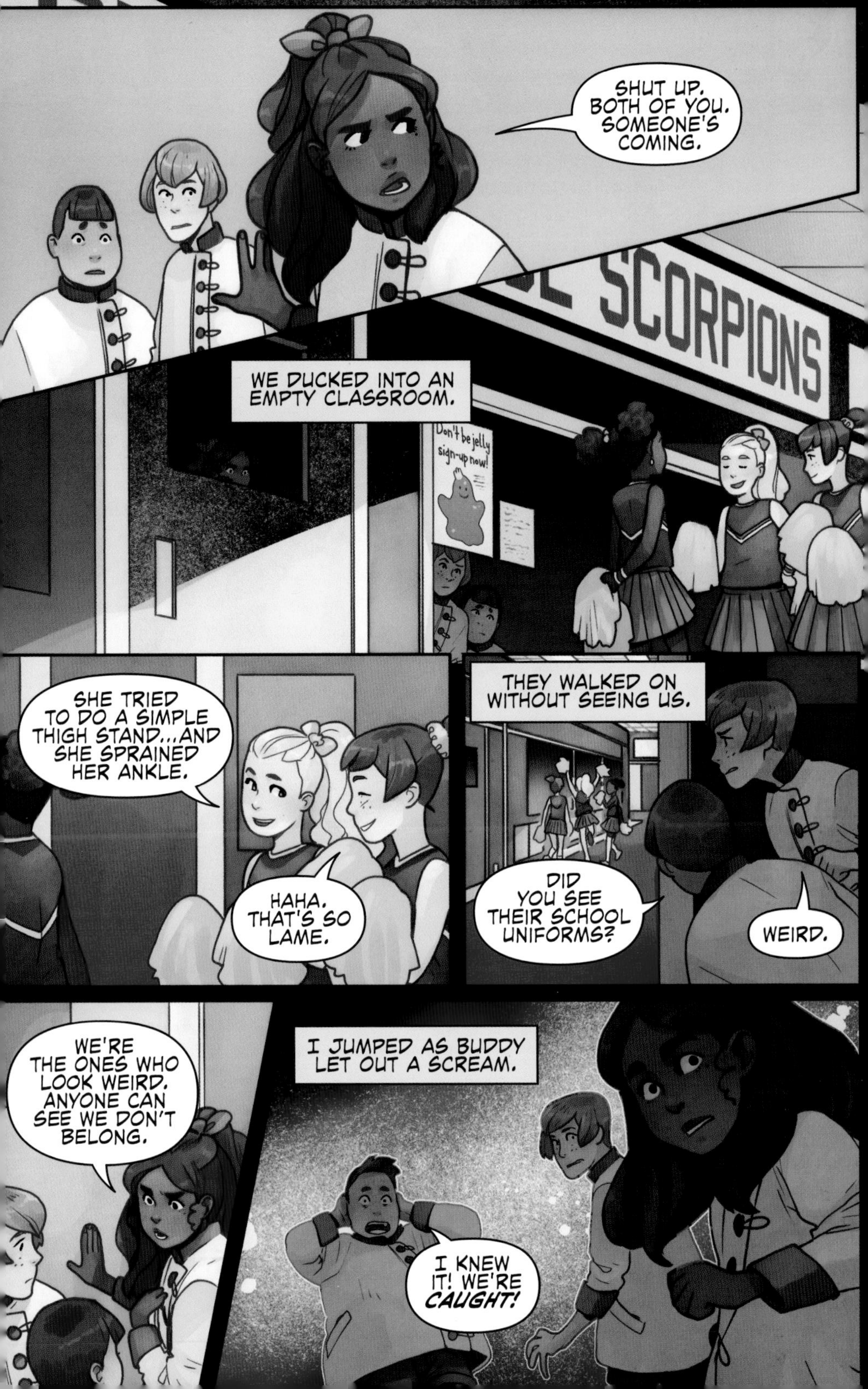
SHUT UP. BOTH OF YOU. SOMEONE'S COMING.
SCORPIONS
WE DUCKED INTO AN EMPTY CLASSROOM.
Don't be jelly sign-up now!
SHE TRIED TO DO A SIMPLE THIGH STAND...AND SHE SPRAINED HER ANKLE.
HAHA. THAT'S SO LAME.
THEY WALKED ON WITHOUT SEEING US.
DID YOU SEE THEIR SCHOOL UNIFORMS?
WEIRD.
WE'RE THE ONES WHO LOOK WEIRD. ANYONE CAN SEE WE DON'T BELONG.
I JUMPED AS BUDDY LET OUT A SCREAM.
I KNEW IT! WE'RE *CAUGHT!*

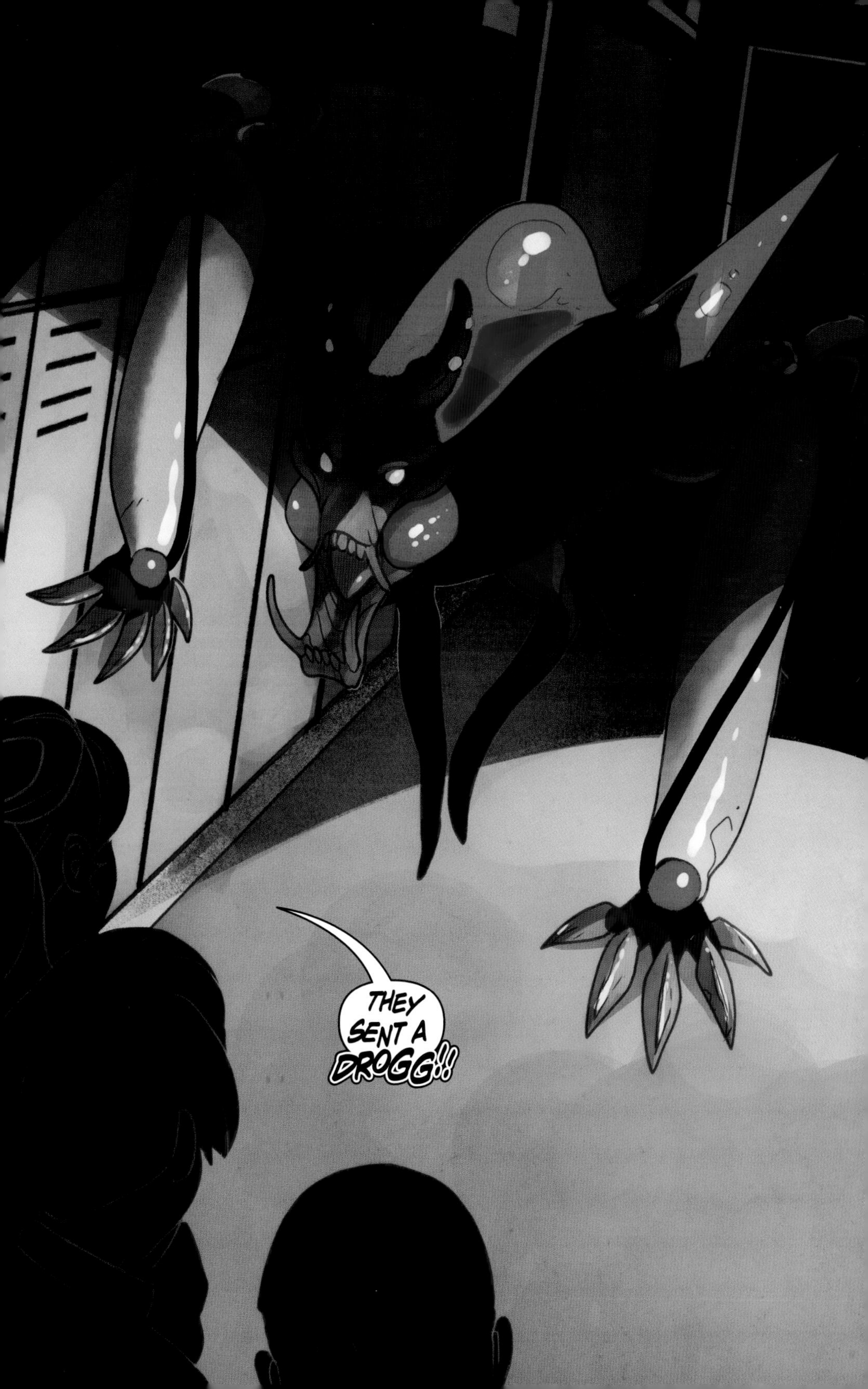
THEY SENT A DROGG!!

CHAPTER TWO
SAVED BY THE BELL

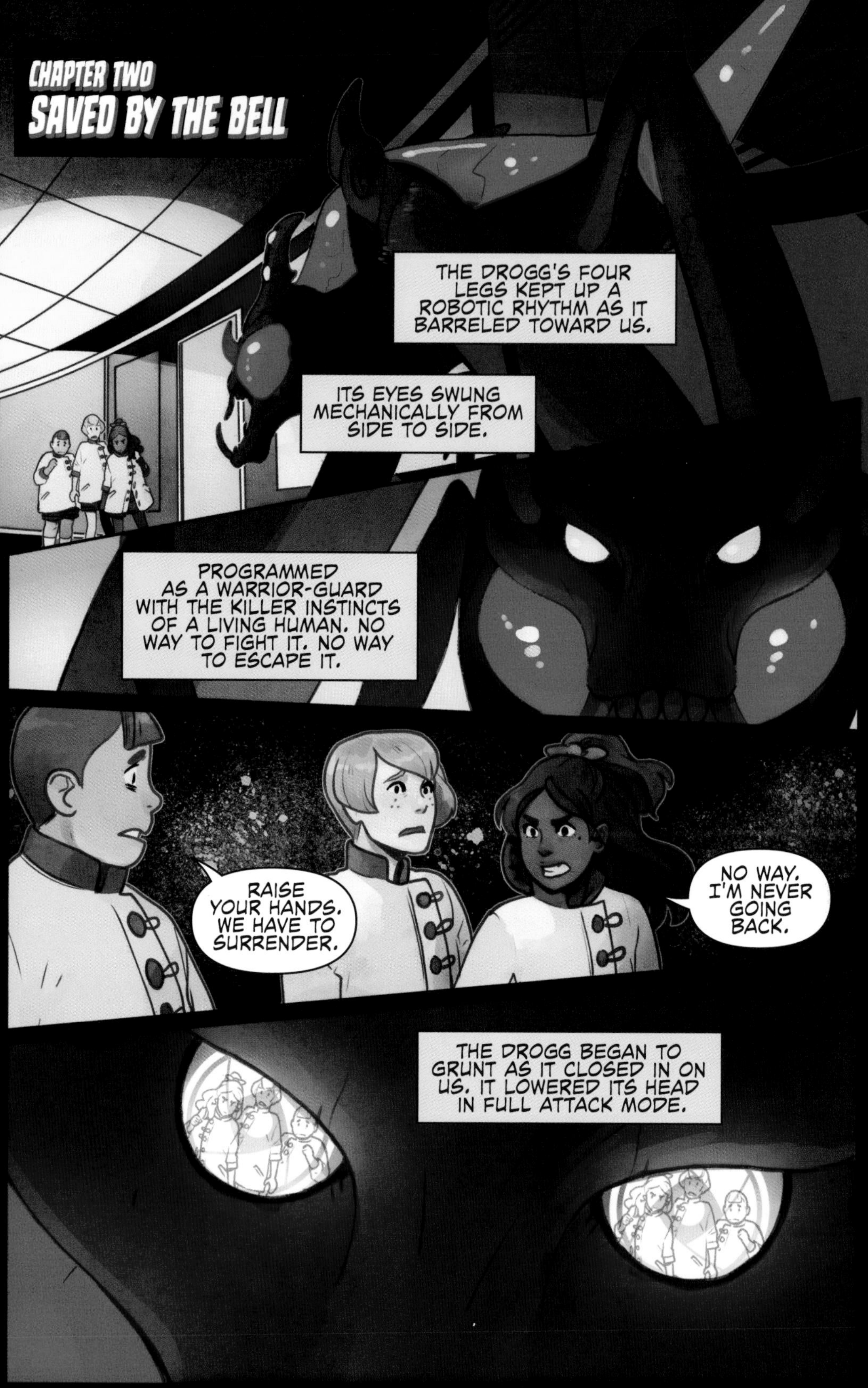
THE DROGG'S FOUR LEGS KEPT UP A ROBOTIC RHYTHM AS IT BARRELED TOWARD US.
ITS EYES SWUNG MECHANICALLY FROM SIDE TO SIDE.
PROGRAMMED AS A WARRIOR-GUARD WITH THE KILLER INSTINCTS OF A LIVING HUMAN. NO WAY TO FIGHT IT. NO WAY TO ESCAPE IT.
RAISE YOUR HANDS. WE HAVE TO SURRENDER.
NO WAY. I'M NEVER GOING BACK.
THE DROGG BEGAN TO GRUNT AS IT CLOSED IN ON US. IT LOWERED ITS HEAD IN FULL ATTACK MODE.

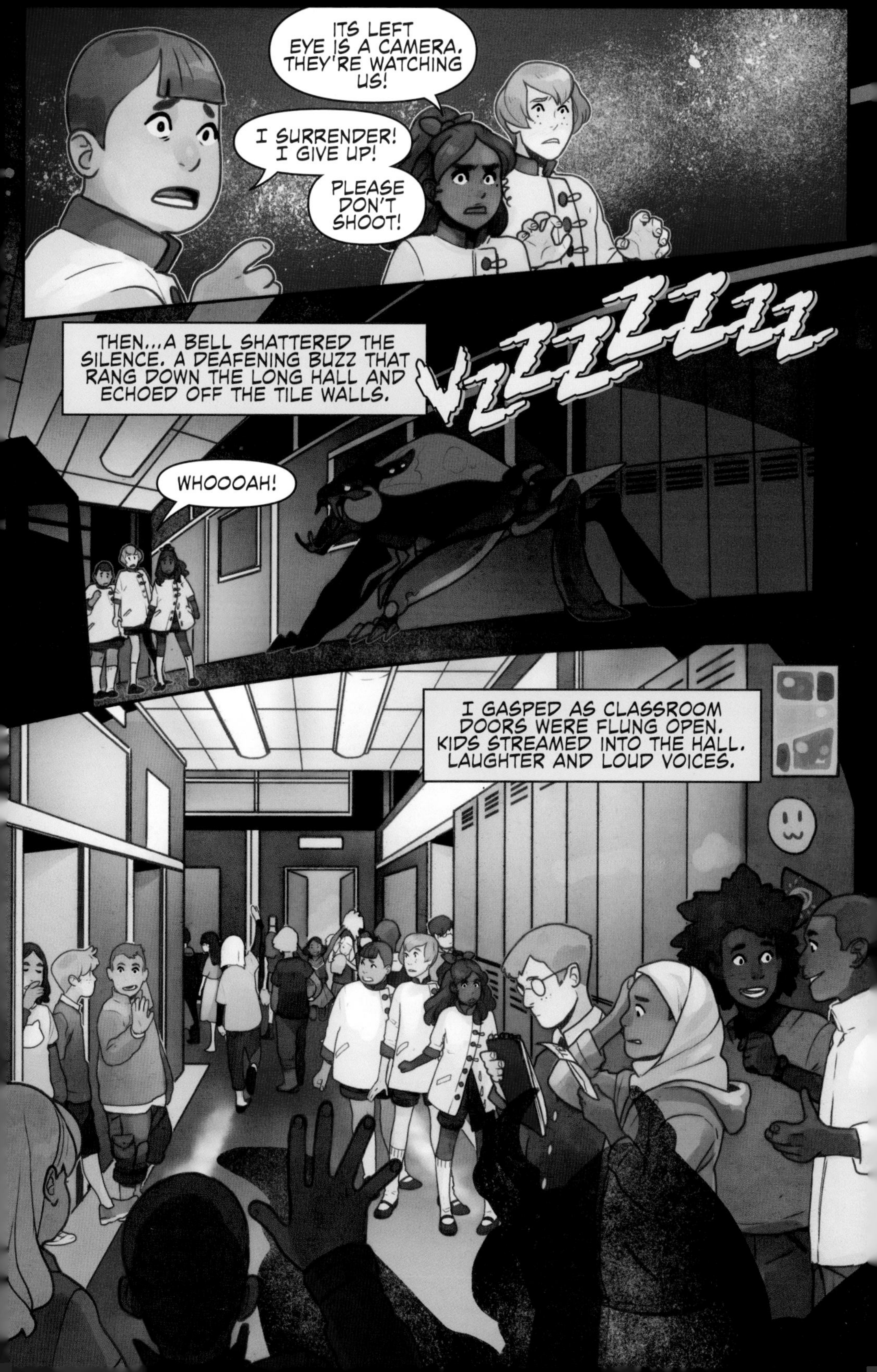
ITS LEFT EYE IS A CAMERA. THEY'RE WATCHING US!
I SURRENDER! I GIVE UP!
PLEASE DON'T SHOOT!
THEN...A BELL SHATTERED THE SILENCE. A DEAFENING BUZZ THAT RANG DOWN THE LONG HALL AND ECHOED OFF THE TILE WALLS.
VZZZZZZZZZ
WHOOOAH!
I GASPED AS CLASSROOM DOORS WERE FLUNG OPEN. KIDS STREAMED INTO THE HALL. LAUGHTER AND LOUD VOICES.

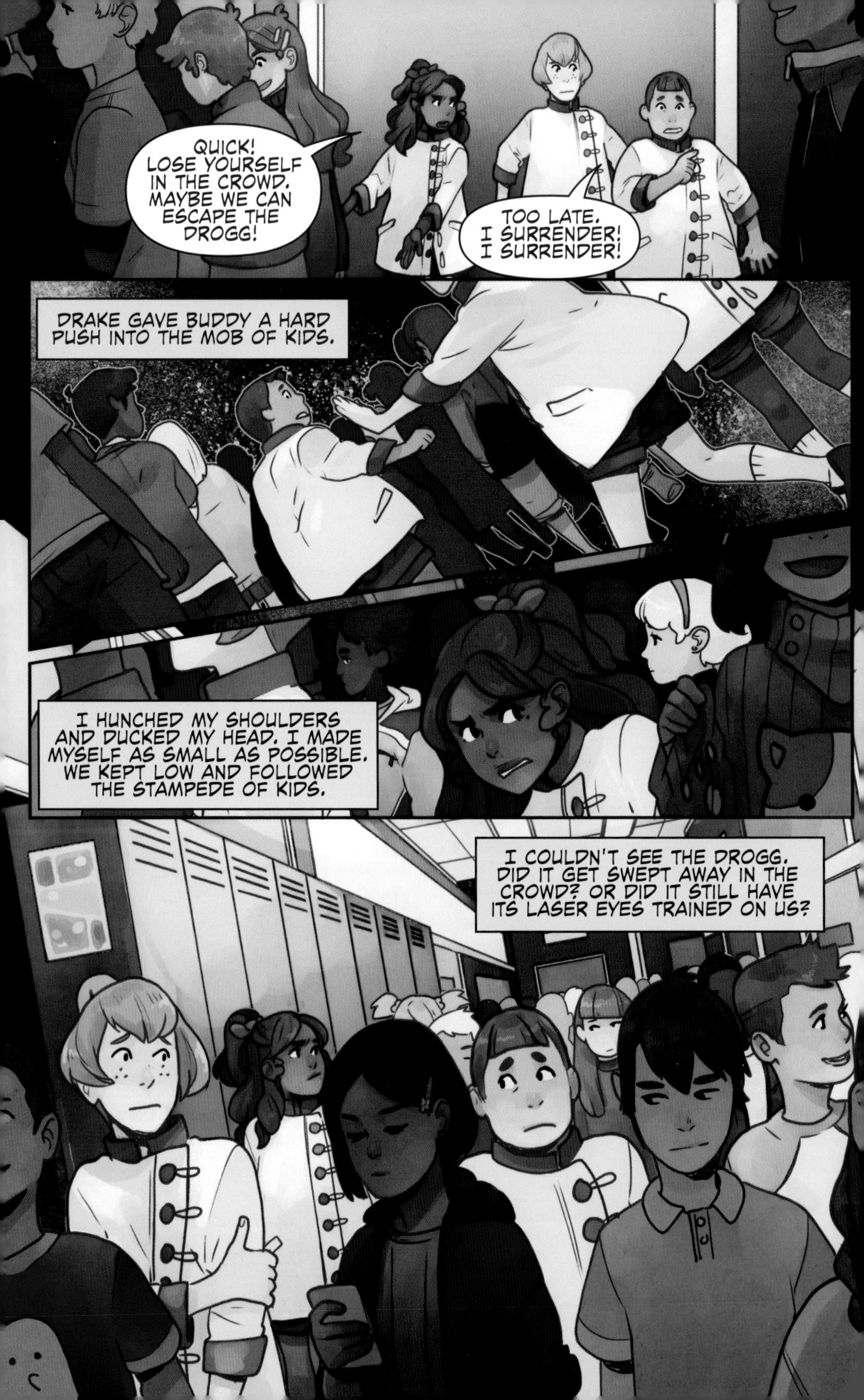
QUICK! LOSE YOURSELF IN THE CROWD. MAYBE WE CAN ESCAPE THE DROGG!
TOO LATE. I SURRENDER! I SURRENDER!
DRAKE GAVE BUDDY A HARD PUSH INTO THE MOB OF KIDS.
I HUNCHED MY SHOULDERS AND DUCKED MY HEAD. I MADE MYSELF AS SMALL AS POSSIBLE. WE KEPT LOW AND FOLLOWED THE STAMPEDE OF KIDS.
I COULDN'T SEE THE DROGG. DID IT GET SWEPT AWAY IN THE CROWD? OR DID IT STILL HAVE ITS LASER EYES TRAINED ON US?

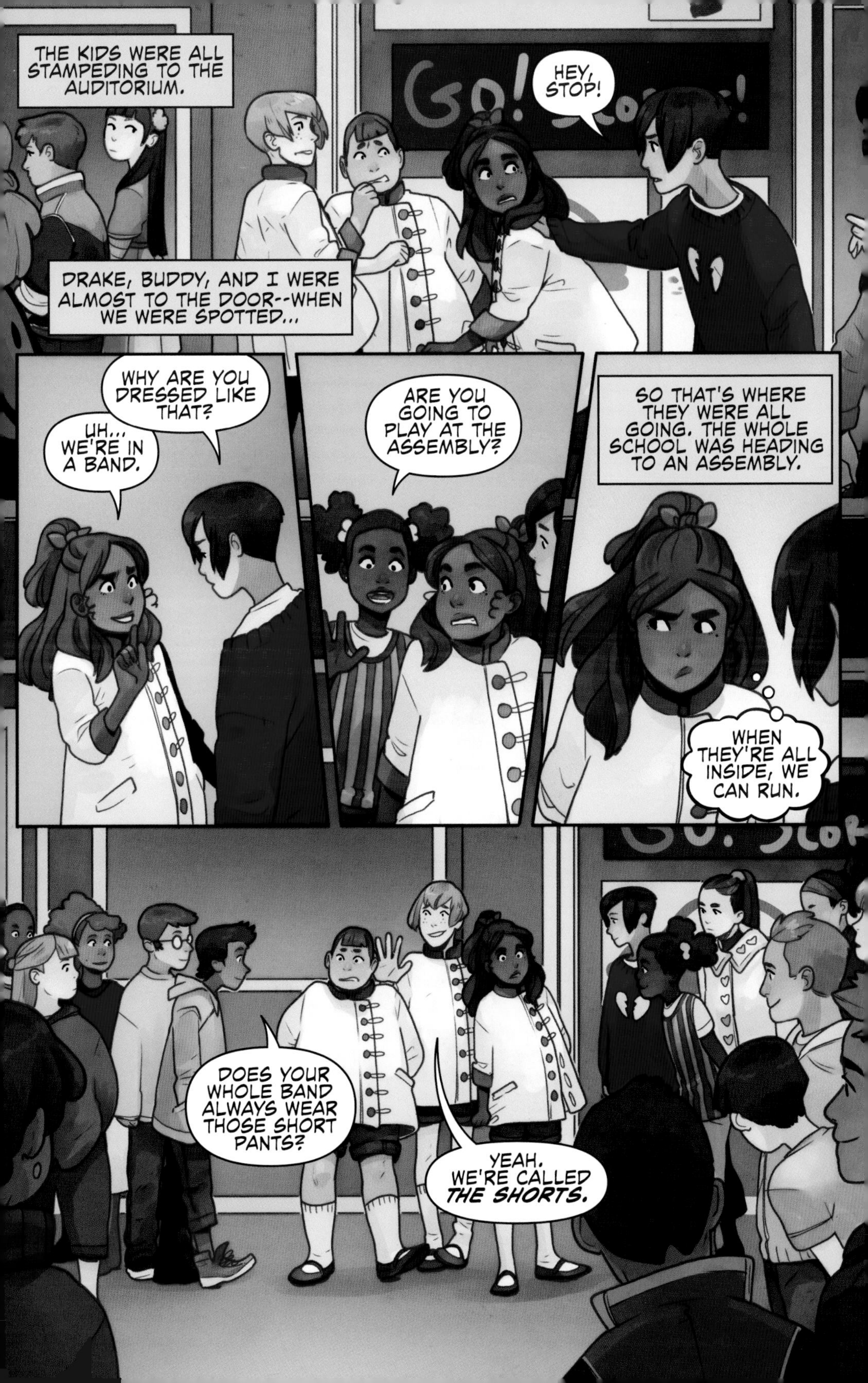
THE KIDS WERE ALL STAMPEDING TO THE AUDITORIUM.
HEY, STOP!
DRAKE, BUDDY, AND I WERE ALMOST TO THE DOOR--WHEN WE WERE SPOTTED...
WHY ARE YOU DRESSED LIKE THAT?
UH... WE'RE IN A BAND.
ARE YOU GOING TO PLAY AT THE ASSEMBLY?
SO THAT'S WHERE THEY WERE ALL GOING. THE WHOLE SCHOOL WAS HEADING TO AN ASSEMBLY.
WHEN THEY'RE ALL INSIDE, WE CAN RUN.
DOES YOUR WHOLE BAND ALWAYS WEAR THOSE SHORT PANTS?
YEAH. WE'RE CALLED *THE SHORTS.*

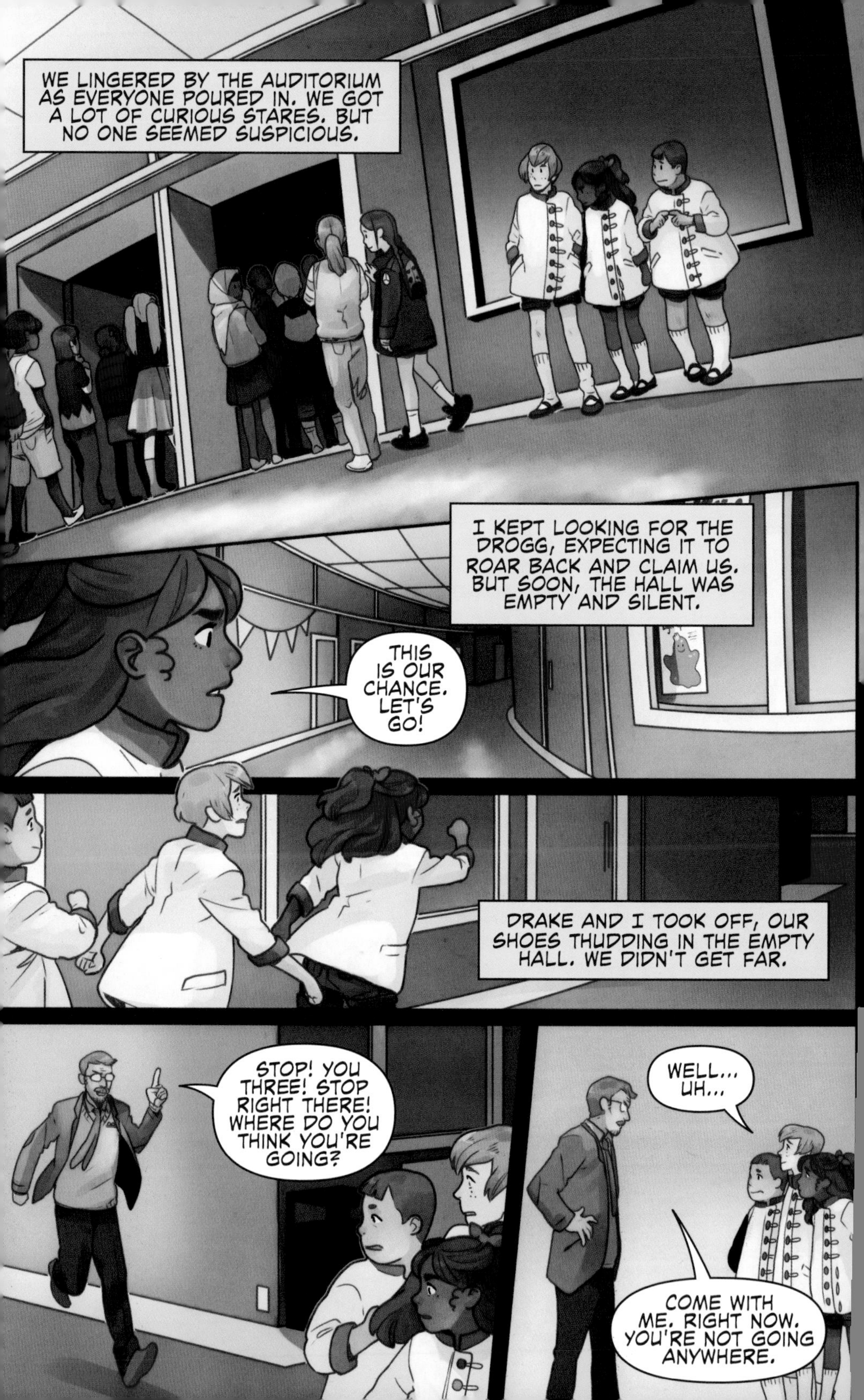
WE LINGERED BY THE AUDITORIUM AS EVERYONE POURED IN. WE GOT A LOT OF CURIOUS STARES. BUT NO ONE SEEMED SUSPICIOUS.
I KEPT LOOKING FOR THE DROGG, EXPECTING IT TO ROAR BACK AND CLAIM US. BUT SOON, THE HALL WAS EMPTY AND SILENT.
THIS IS OUR CHANCE. LET'S GO!
DRAKE AND I TOOK OFF, OUR SHOES THUDDING IN THE EMPTY HALL. WE DIDN'T GET FAR.
STOP! YOU THREE! STOP RIGHT THERE! WHERE DO YOU THINK YOU'RE GOING?
WELL... UH...
COME WITH ME. RIGHT NOW. YOU'RE NOT GOING ANYWHERE.

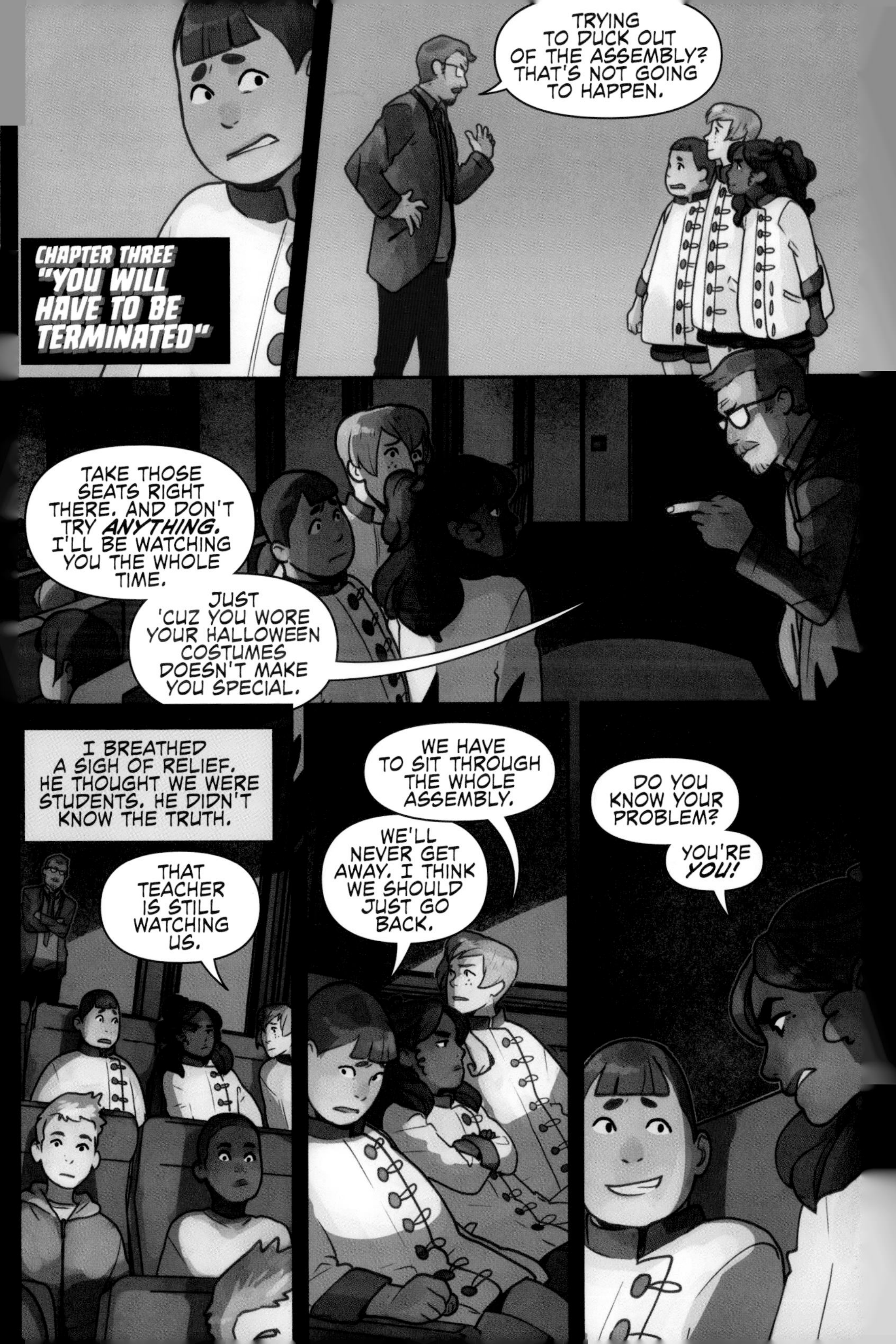
CHAPTER THREE "YOU WILL HAVE TO BE TERMINATED"
TRYING TO DUCK OUT OF THE ASSEMBLY? THAT'S NOT GOING TO HAPPEN.
TAKE THOSE SEATS RIGHT THERE. AND DON'T TRY ANYTHING. I'LL BE WATCHING YOU THE WHOLE TIME.
JUST 'CUZ YOU WORE YOUR HALLOWEEN COSTUMES DOESN'T MAKE YOU SPECIAL.
I BREATHED A SIGH OF RELIEF. HE THOUGHT WE WERE STUDENTS. HE DIDN'T KNOW THE TRUTH.
THAT TEACHER IS STILL WATCHING US.
WE HAVE TO SIT THROUGH THE WHOLE ASSEMBLY.
WE'LL NEVER GET AWAY. I THINK WE SHOULD JUST GO BACK.
DO YOU KNOW YOUR PROBLEM?
YOU'RE YOU!

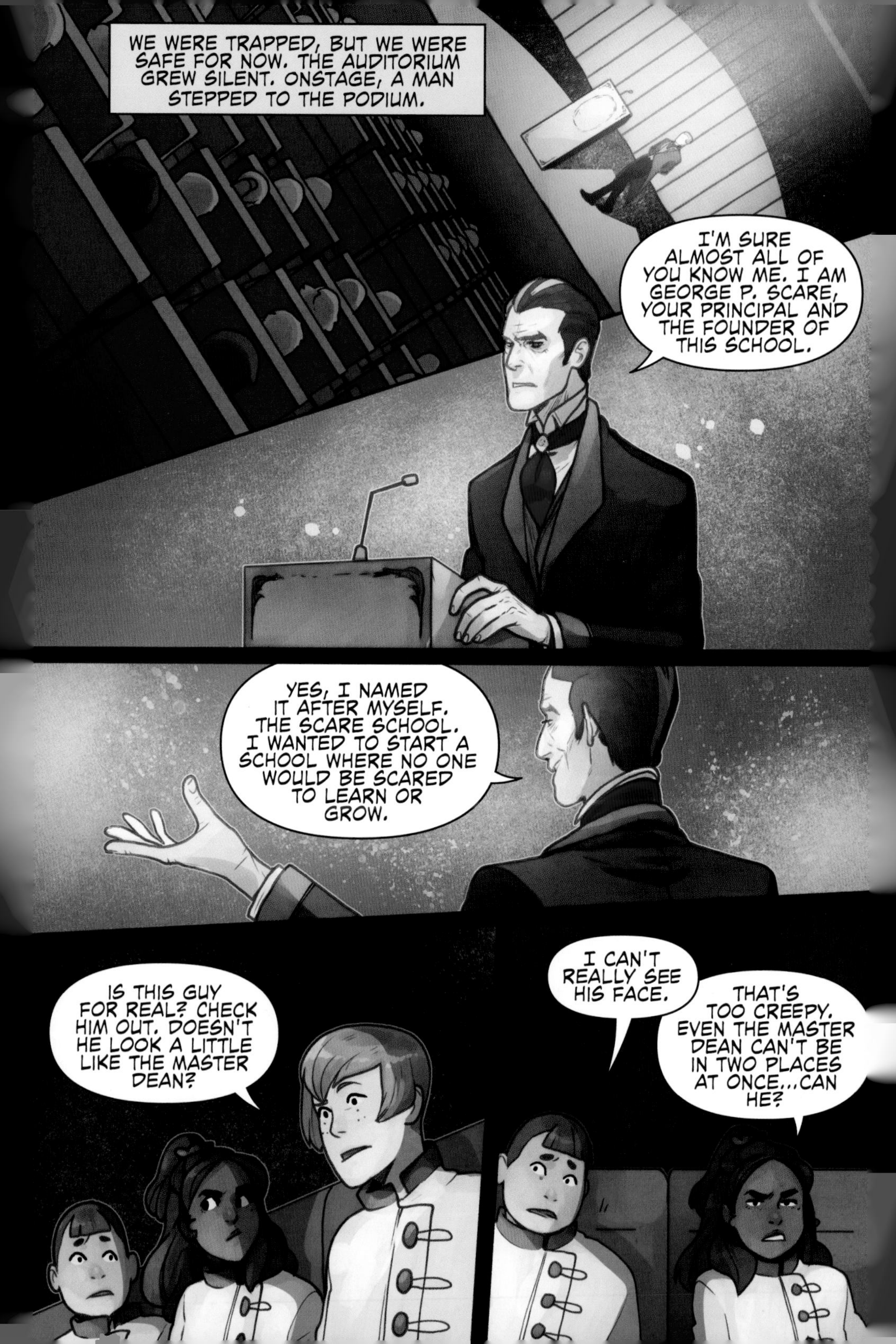
WE WERE TRAPPED, BUT WE WERE SAFE FOR NOW. THE AUDITORIUM GREW SILENT. ONSTAGE, A MAN STEPPED TO THE PODIUM.
I'M SURE ALMOST ALL OF YOU KNOW ME. I AM GEORGE P. SCARE, YOUR PRINCIPAL AND THE FOUNDER OF THIS SCHOOL.
YES, I NAMED IT AFTER MYSELF. THE SCARE SCHOOL. I WANTED TO START A SCHOOL WHERE NO ONE WOULD BE SCARED TO LEARN OR GROW.
IS THIS GUY FOR REAL? CHECK HIM OUT. DOESN'T HE LOOK A LITTLE LIKE THE MASTER DEAN?
I CAN'T REALLY SEE HIS FACE.
THAT'S TOO CREEPY. EVEN THE MASTER DEAN CAN'T BE IN TWO PLACES AT ONCE...CAN HE?

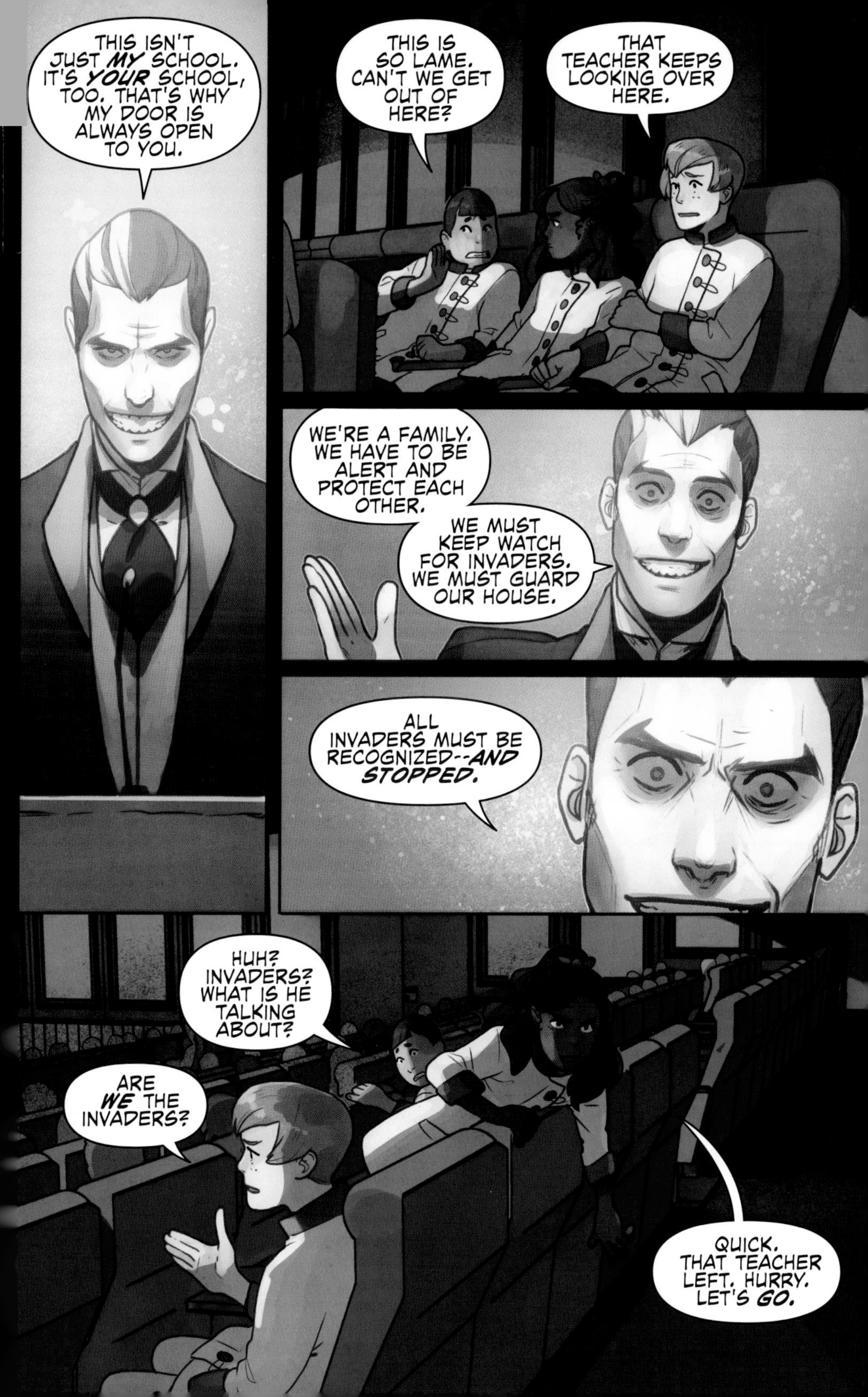
THIS ISN'T JUST *MY* SCHOOL. IT'S *YOUR* SCHOOL, TOO. THAT'S WHY MY DOOR IS ALWAYS OPEN TO YOU.
THIS IS SO LAME. CAN'T WE GET OUT OF HERE?
THAT TEACHER KEEPS LOOKING OVER HERE.
WE'RE A FAMILY. WE HAVE TO BE ALERT AND PROTECT EACH OTHER.
WE MUST KEEP WATCH FOR INVADERS. WE MUST GUARD OUR HOUSE.
ALL INVADERS MUST BE RECOGNIZED--*AND STOPPED.*
HUH? INVADERS? WHAT IS HE TALKING ABOUT?
ARE *WE* THE INVADERS?
QUICK. THAT TEACHER LEFT. HURRY. LET'S *GO.*

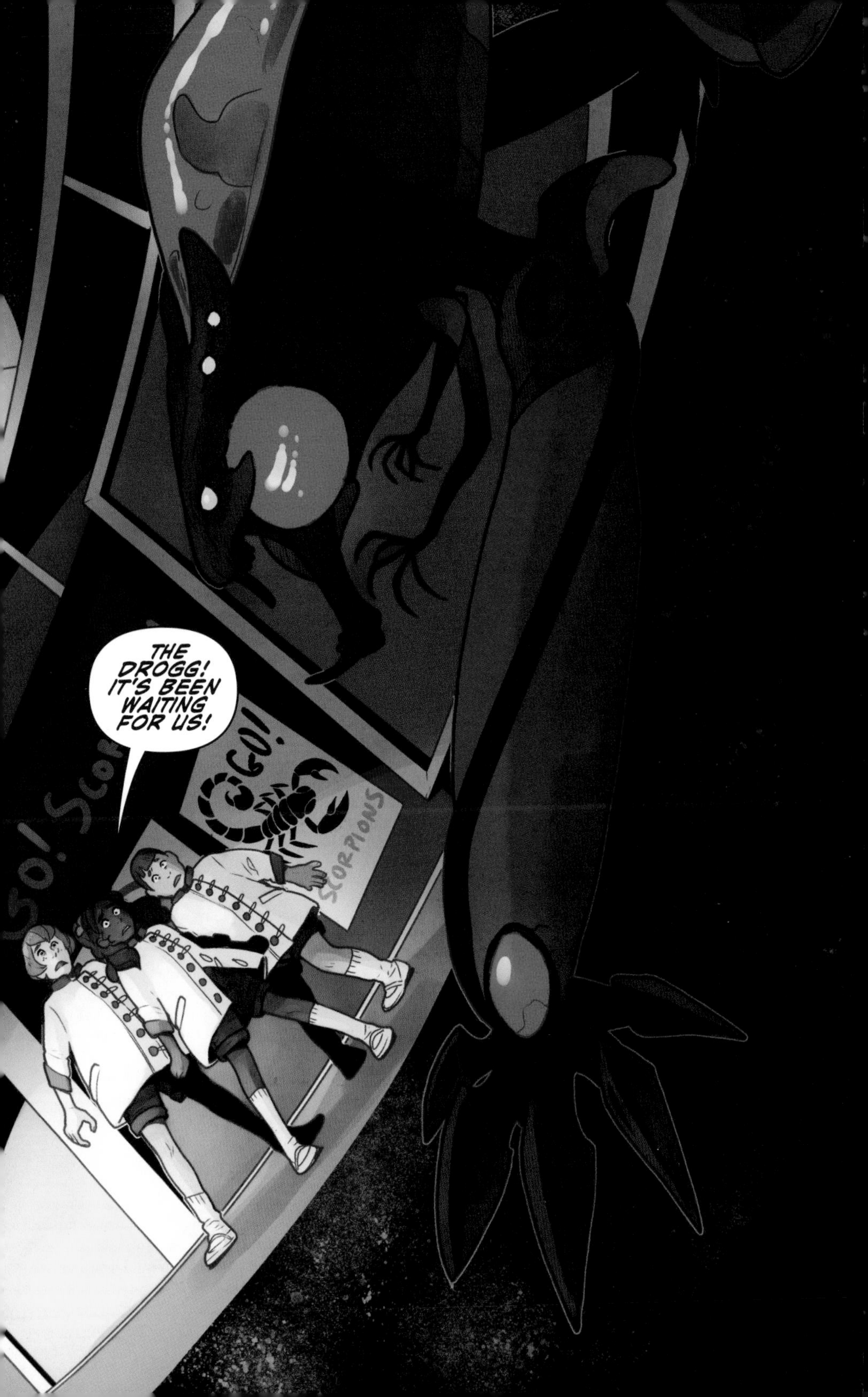
THE DROGG! IT'S BEEN WAITING FOR US!
GO!
SCORPIONS

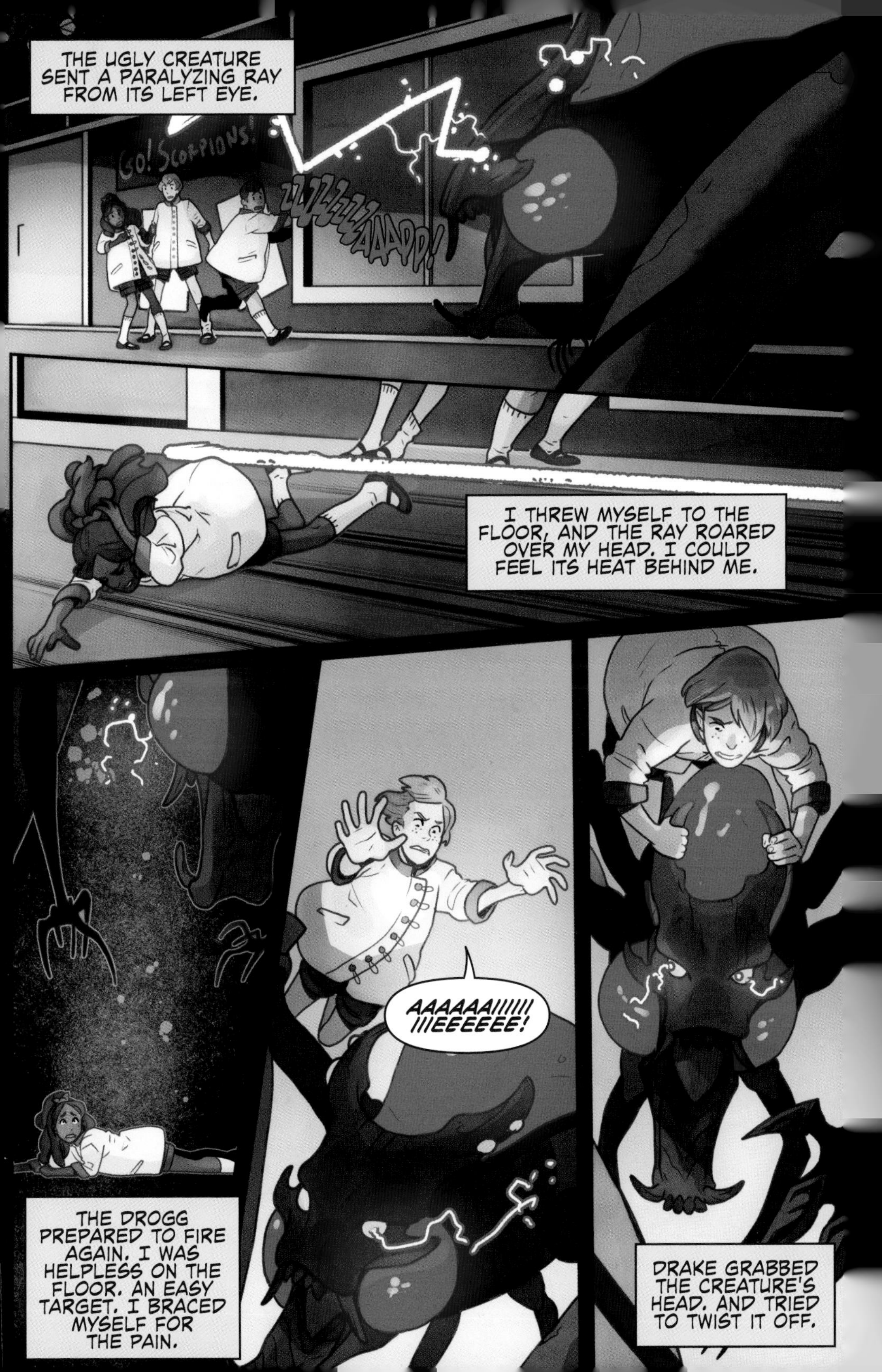
THE UGLY CREATURE SENT A PARALYZING RAY FROM ITS LEFT EYE.
GO! SCORPIONS!
ZZZZZZZZAAADD!
I THREW MYSELF TO THE FLOOR, AND THE RAY ROARED OVER MY HEAD. I COULD FEEL ITS HEAT BEHIND ME.
THE DROGG PREPARED TO FIRE AGAIN. I WAS HELPLESS ON THE FLOOR. AN EASY TARGET. I BRACED MYSELF FOR THE PAIN.
AAAAAAIIIIIIIIIEEEEEEE!
DRAKE GRABBED THE CREATURE'S HEAD, AND TRIED TO TWIST IT OFF.

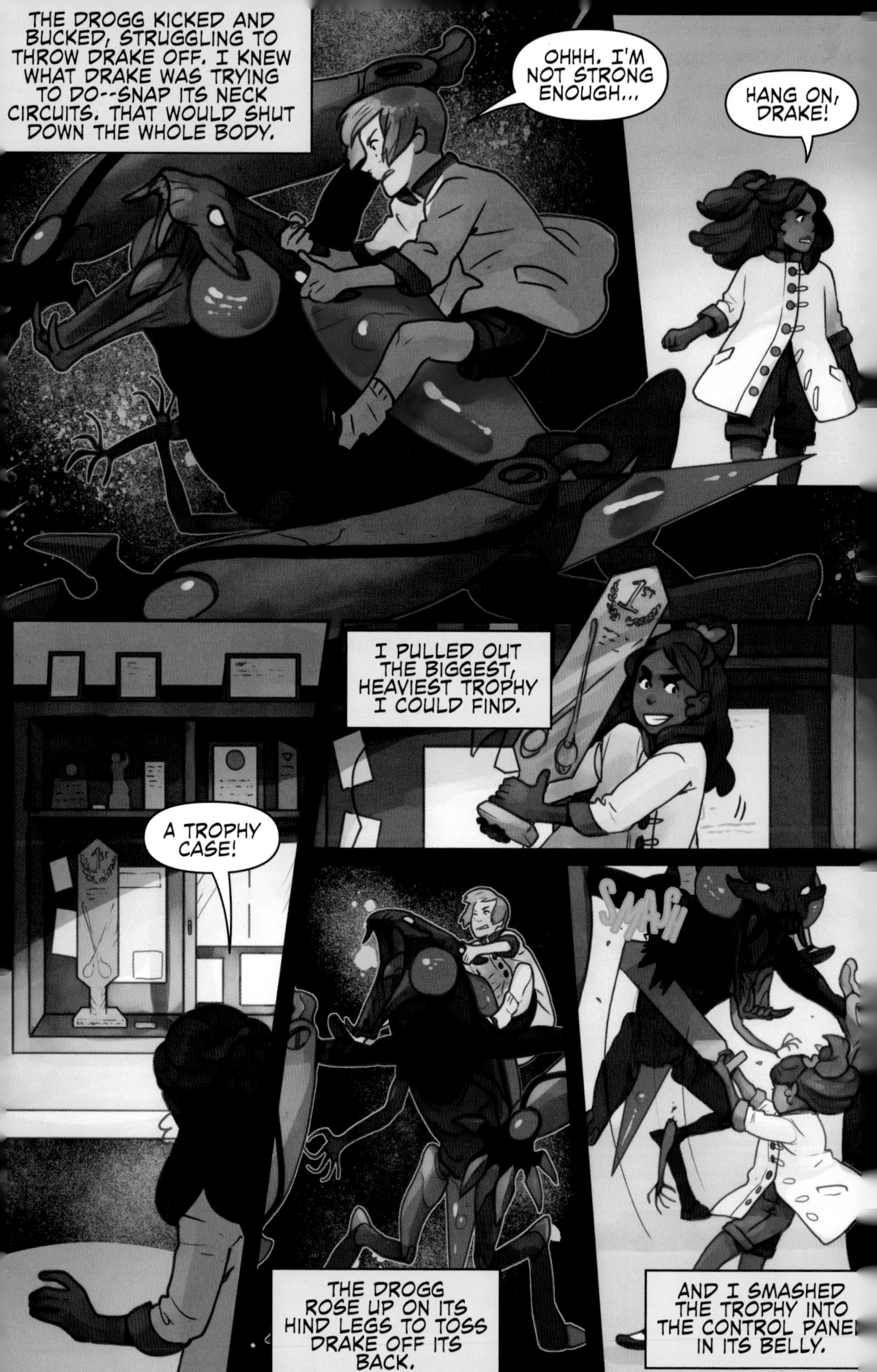
THE DROGG KICKED AND BUCKED, STRUGGLING TO THROW DRAKE OFF. I KNEW WHAT DRAKE WAS TRYING TO DO--SNAP ITS NECK CIRCUITS. THAT WOULD SHUT DOWN THE WHOLE BODY.
OHHH. I'M NOT STRONG ENOUGH...
HANG ON, DRAKE!
A TROPHY CASE!
I PULLED OUT THE BIGGEST, HEAVIEST TROPHY I COULD FIND.
THE DROGG ROSE UP ON ITS HIND LEGS TO TOSS DRAKE OFF ITS BACK.
SMASH
AND I SMASHED THE TROPHY INTO THE CONTROL PANEL IN ITS BELLY.

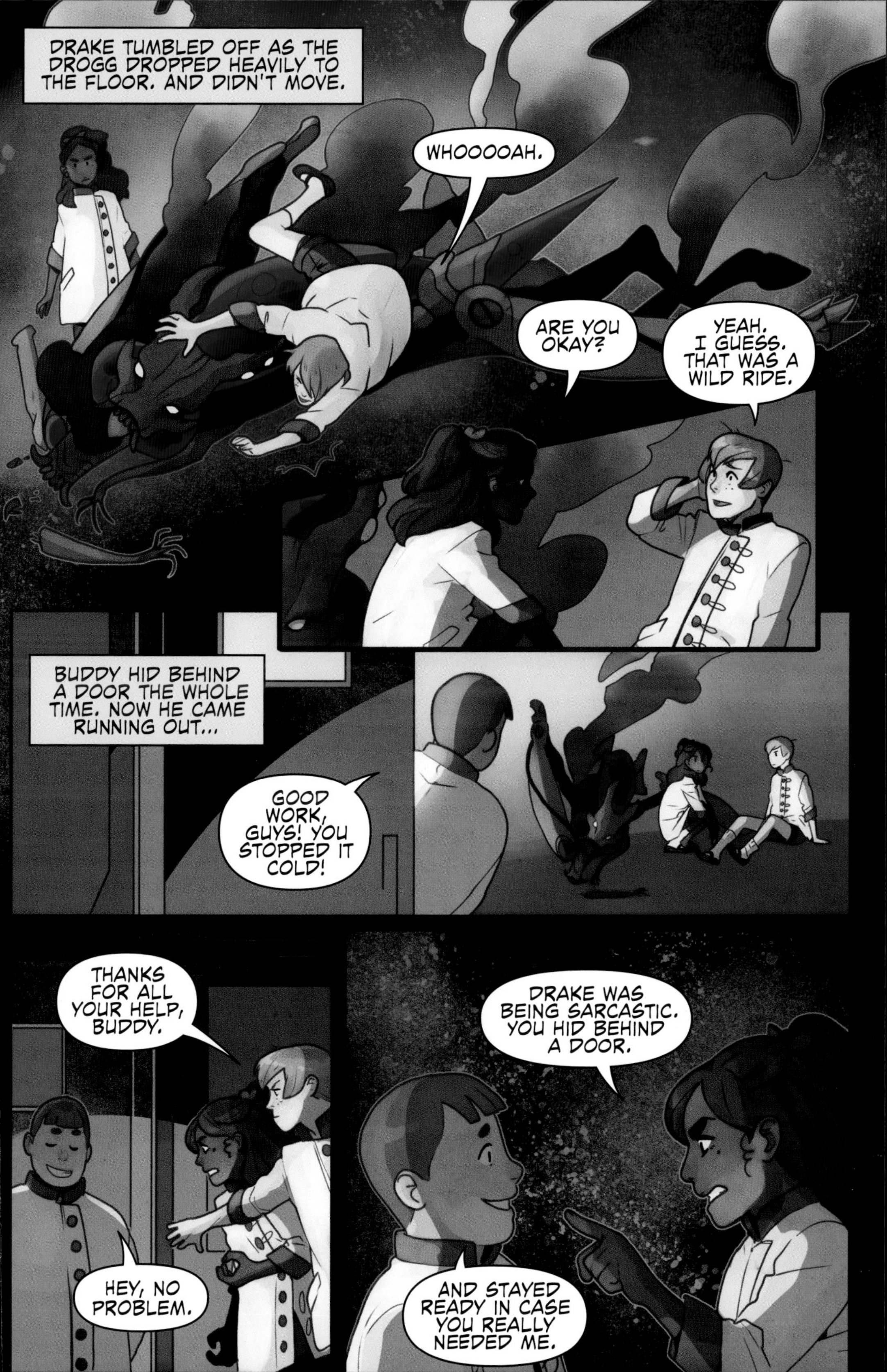
DRAKE TUMBLED OFF AS THE DROGG DROPPED HEAVILY TO THE FLOOR. AND DIDN'T MOVE.
WHOOOOAH.
ARE YOU OKAY?
YEAH. I GUESS. THAT WAS A WILD RIDE.
BUDDY HID BEHIND A DOOR THE WHOLE TIME. NOW HE CAME RUNNING OUT...
GOOD WORK, GUYS! YOU STOPPED IT COLD!
THANKS FOR ALL YOUR HELP, BUDDY.
HEY, NO PROBLEM.
DRAKE WAS BEING SARCASTIC. YOU HID BEHIND A DOOR.
AND STAYED READY IN CASE YOU REALLY NEEDED ME.

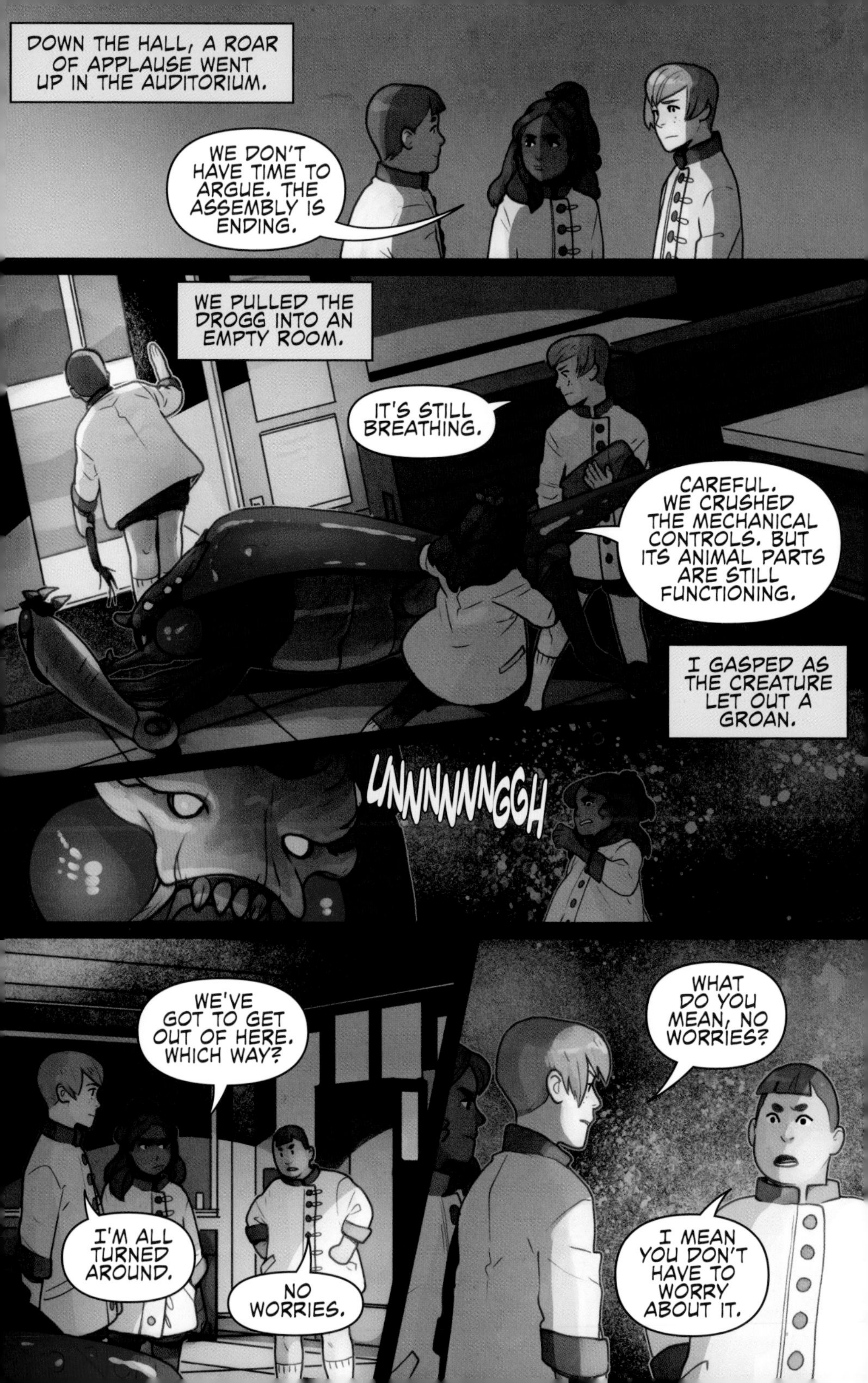
DOWN THE HALL, A ROAR OF APPLAUSE WENT UP IN THE AUDITORIUM.
WE DON'T HAVE TIME TO ARGUE. THE ASSEMBLY IS ENDING.
WE PULLED THE DROGG INTO AN EMPTY ROOM.
IT'S STILL BREATHING.
CAREFUL. WE CRUSHED THE MECHANICAL CONTROLS. BUT ITS ANIMAL PARTS ARE STILL FUNCTIONING.
I GASPED AS THE CREATURE LET OUT A GROAN.
UNNNNNNGGH
WE'VE GOT TO GET OUT OF HERE. WHICH WAY?
I'M ALL TURNED AROUND.
NO WORRIES.
WHAT DO YOU MEAN, NO WORRIES?
I MEAN YOU DON'T HAVE TO WORRY ABOUT IT.

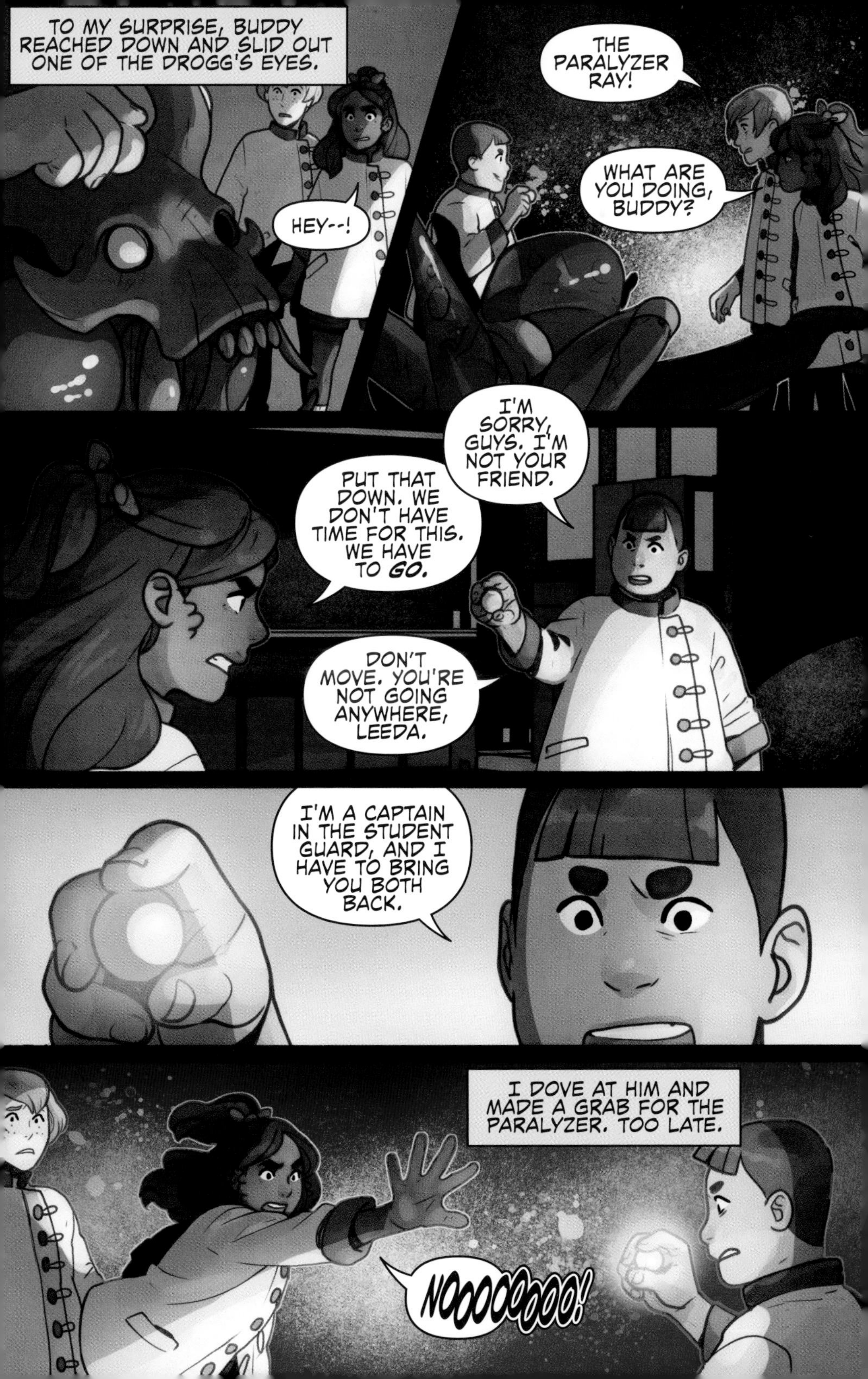
TO MY SURPRISE, BUDDY REACHED DOWN AND SLID OUT ONE OF THE DROGG'S EYES.
HEY--!
THE PARALYZER RAY!
WHAT ARE YOU DOING, BUDDY?
I'M SORRY, GUYS. I'M NOT YOUR FRIEND.
PUT THAT DOWN. WE DON'T HAVE TIME FOR THIS. WE HAVE TO GO.
DON'T MOVE. YOU'RE NOT GOING ANYWHERE, LEEDA.
I'M A CAPTAIN IN THE STUDENT GUARD, AND I HAVE TO BRING YOU BOTH BACK.
I DOVE AT HIM AND MADE A GRAB FOR THE PARALYZER. TOO LATE.
NOOOOOOOO!

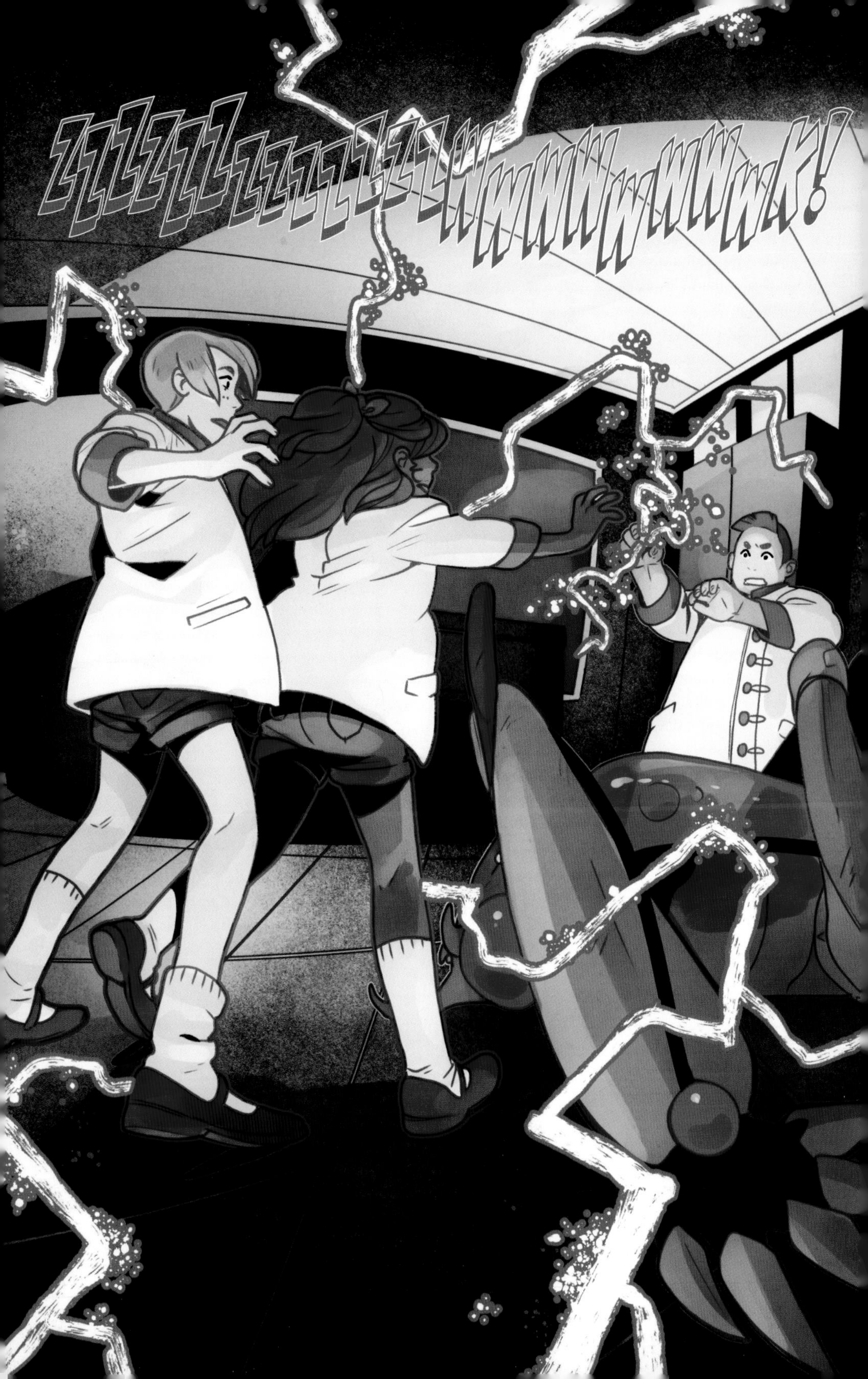
ZZZZZZzzzzZZZZWWWWWwWWWWwk!

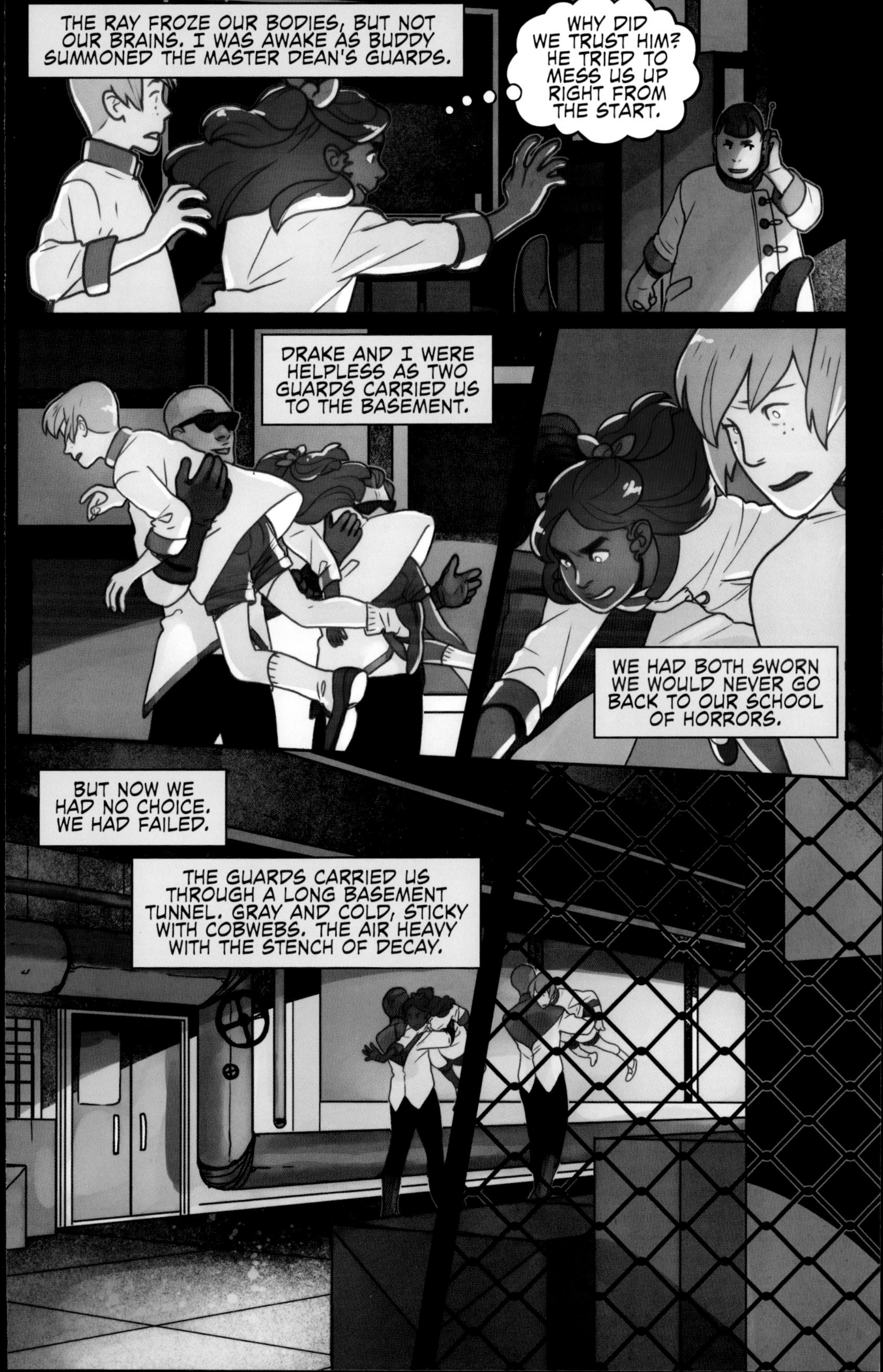
THE RAY FROZE OUR BODIES, BUT NOT OUR BRAINS. I WAS AWAKE AS BUDDY SUMMONED THE MASTER DEAN'S GUARDS.
WHY DID WE TRUST HIM? HE TRIED TO MESS US UP RIGHT FROM THE START.
DRAKE AND I WERE HELPLESS AS TWO GUARDS CARRIED US TO THE BASEMENT.
WE HAD BOTH SWORN WE WOULD NEVER GO BACK TO OUR SCHOOL OF HORRORS.
BUT NOW WE HAD NO CHOICE. WE HAD FAILED.
THE GUARDS CARRIED US THROUGH A LONG BASEMENT TUNNEL. GRAY AND COLD, STICKY WITH COBWEBS. THE AIR HEAVY WITH THE STENCH OF DECAY.

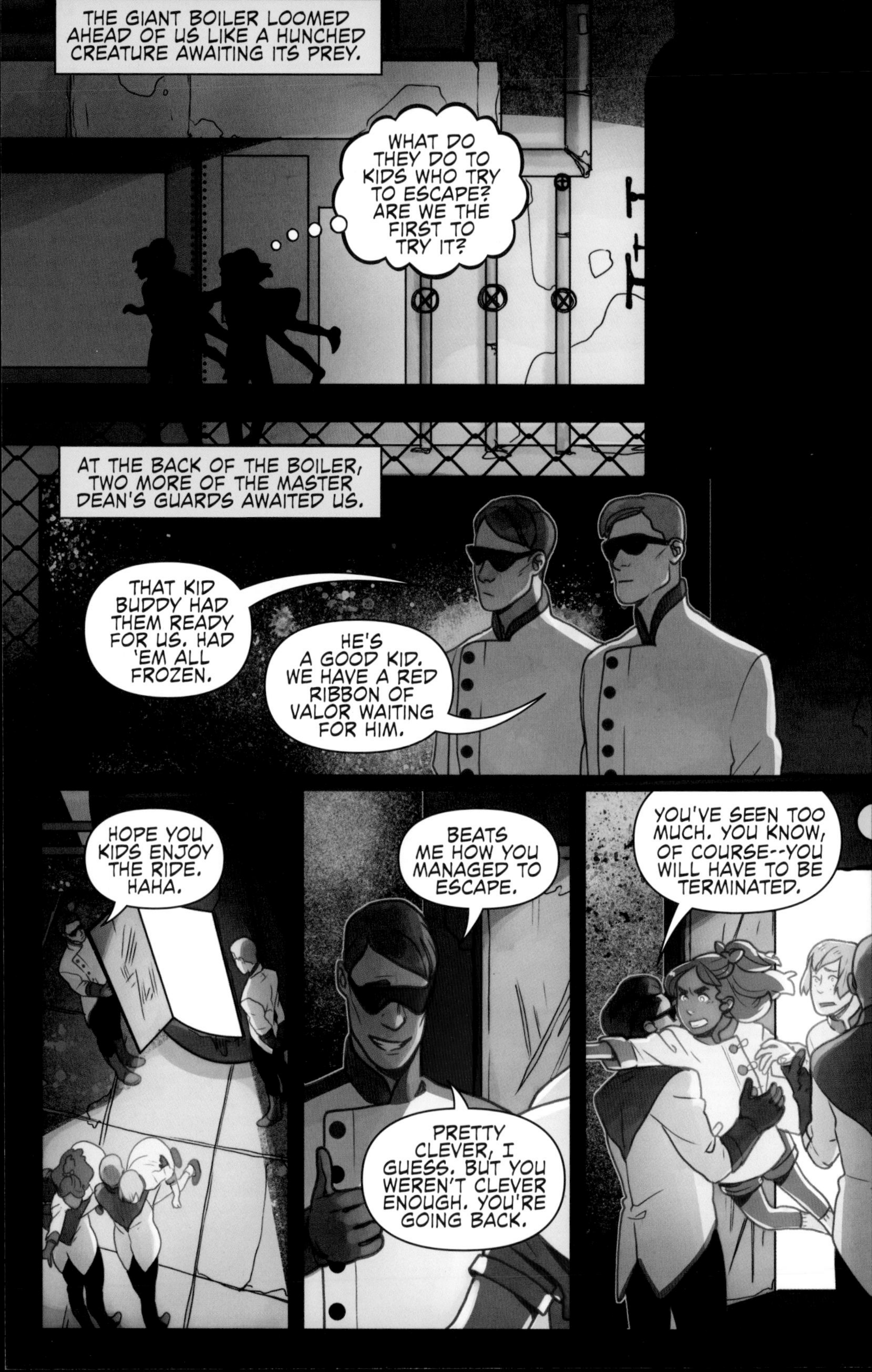
THE GIANT BOILER LOOMED AHEAD OF US LIKE A HUNCHED CREATURE AWAITING ITS PREY.
WHAT DO THEY DO TO KIDS WHO TRY TO ESCAPE? ARE WE THE FIRST TO TRY IT?
AT THE BACK OF THE BOILER, TWO MORE OF THE MASTER DEAN'S GUARDS AWAITED US.
THAT KID BUDDY HAD THEM READY FOR US. HAD 'EM ALL FROZEN.
HE'S A GOOD KID. WE HAVE A RED RIBBON OF VALOR WAITING FOR HIM.
HOPE YOU KIDS ENJOY THE RIDE. HAHA.
BEATS ME HOW YOU MANAGED TO ESCAPE.
PRETTY CLEVER, I GUESS. BUT YOU WEREN'T CLEVER ENOUGH. YOU'RE GOING BACK.
YOU'VE SEEN TOO MUCH. YOU KNOW, OF COURSE--YOU WILL HAVE TO BE TERMINATED.

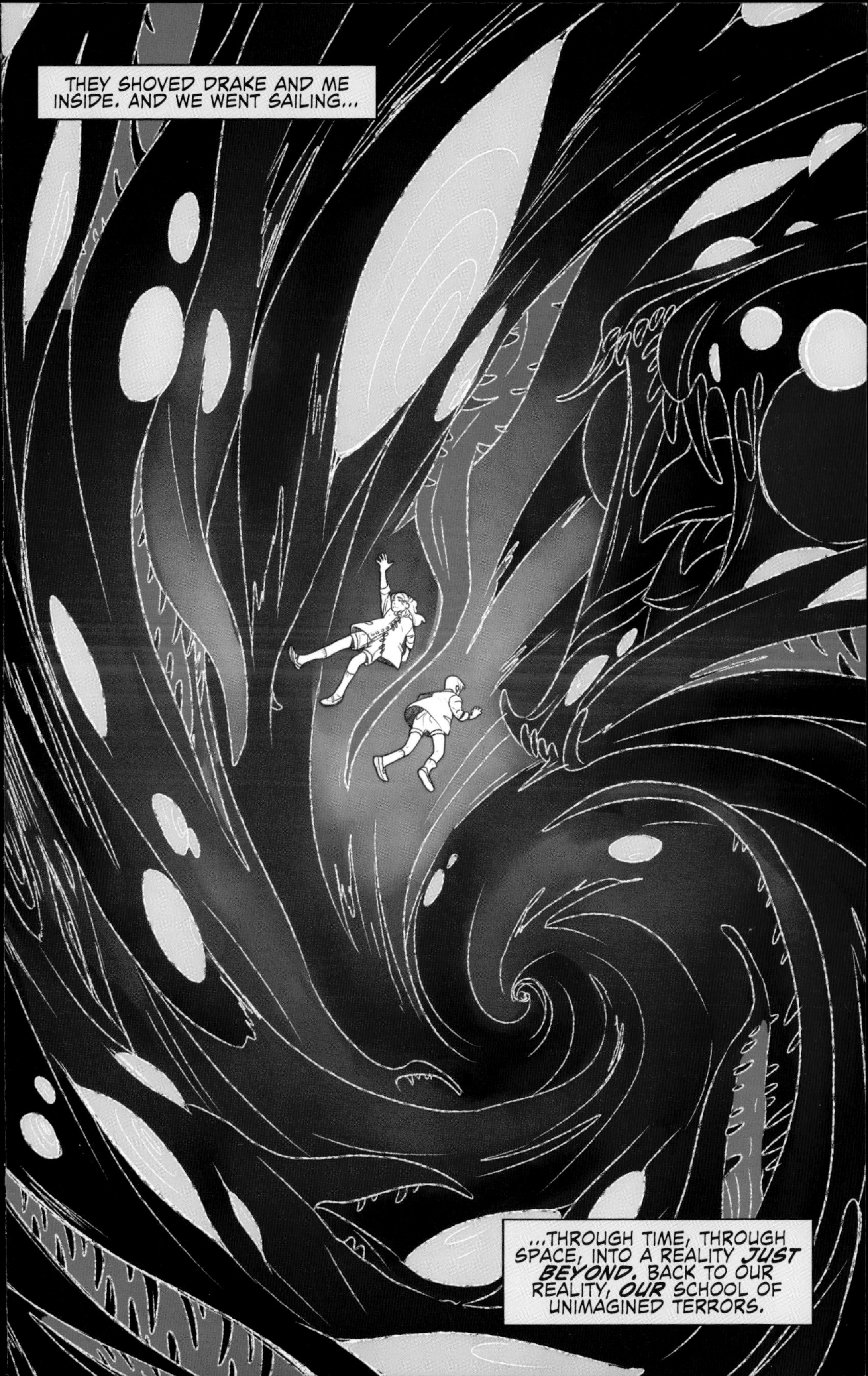
THEY SHOVED DRAKE AND ME INSIDE. AND WE WENT SAILING...
...THROUGH TIME, THROUGH SPACE, INTO A REALITY *JUST BEYOND.* BACK TO OUR REALITY, *OUR* SCHOOL OF UNIMAGINED TERRORS.

JUST BEYOND™

COLLECT THEM ALL!

Set of 4 Hardcover Books ISBN: 978-1-5321-4488-2

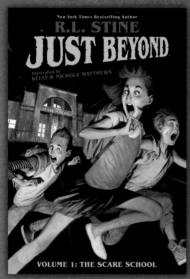

Hardcover Book ISBN
978-1-5321-4489-9

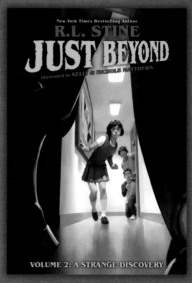

Hardcover Book ISBN
978-1-5321-4490-5

Hardcover Book ISBN
978-1-5321-4491-2

Hardcover Book ISBN
978-1-5321-4492-9